Mathematics Wizard

SRINIVASA RAMANUJAN

Mathematics Wizard
SRINIVASA RAMANUJAN
Some Glimpses into his Life and Work

Narendra Kumar Govil
Bhu Dev Sharma

Published by
PRABHAT PRAKASHAN PVT. LTD.
4/19 Asaf Ali Road,
New Delhi-110 002 (INDIA)
e-mail: prabhatbooks@gmail.com

ISBN 978-93-90366-73-6
Mathematics Wizard : SRINIVASA RAMANUJAN
by Shri Narendra Kumar Govil • Shri Bhu Dev Sharma

Edition
2025

Price
₹ 500.00 (Rupees Five Hundred only)

Printed at
R-Tech Offset Printers, Delhi

Eberly College of Science
Department of Mathematics
The Pennsylvania State University
University Park, PA 1 6802
(814) 865-7527

Foreword

Srinivasa Ramanujan has been an immense inspiration to many for the last 100 years, and he has been one of the most important influences in my life and career. It greatly pleases me to provide a foreword to this new book by Professors Govil and Sharma. This book is rather short as biographies go, but it is quite complete. It provides a nice complement to the book, The Man Who Knew Infinity, by the American biographer, Robert Kanigel. Now we have a book by two Indian mathematicians that provides an Indian perspective on the life of Ramanujan, and what an amazing story this is. Ramanujan was born in poverty, rose to fame as one of the most profound number theorists of the 20th century, became seriously ill in his twenties, and died at the age of 32. This has all the elements of grand literary tragedy. This book provides a full account of this unbelievable life. In addition, I would especially wish to highlight Chapter 12, Glimpses of Ramanujan's Mathematics, Chapter 13, Legacy of Ramanujan today, and Chapter 14, Reference Material on Ramanujan. This component makes this book a unique contribution to the Ramanujan literature. The book concludes with an appendix devoted to an article by Krishna Alladi, The SASTRA Ramanujan Prize: Its Origins and Its Winners. This book is a welcome reminder not only of the greatness of Ramanujan but also of the many ways he has contributed to the international mathematics community.

Thank you Professors Govil and Sharma.

George

(George E. Andrews)
Evan Pugh University Professor of Mathematics
Member, National Academy of Sciences (USA)
Past President, American Mathematical Society

Preface

Ramanujan is a universally well-known 20th century's one of the most charismatic mathematicians, with a standing and reputation such as only a very few other mathematicians enjoy. His is the inspiring story of a self-made superb mathematician under total adverse conditions. He was a poor, untrained, living example of a divinely inspired person with short life and immense contributions. In a short life of 32 years, he gave a wealth of ideas that continue to shape 21st century mathematics.

There are many books, numerous biographies and countless essays on Ramanujan as are also some films, activities, journals, honors and awards on Ramanujan, listed in Chapters 13 & 14, at the end of the book. Looking at the need of a book about the life of Ramanujan in Hindi, the national language of India, spoken by about 500 million people world wide, we wrote a book in Hindi. This book was published by Prabhat Prakashan, New Delhi, India and first appeared in 2005. The book was very well received in India and abroad with Hindi speaking people, and had several repeated editions. There was a demand, both in India and abroad, to translate this book in English or to write one in English that could serve a world-wide audience. While translation was not possible because of rather obvious reasons, we thought of writing a new book.

As is well-known, India is world's oldest civilization with strong Hindu-Vedic intellectual contributions. Ramanujan was a Brahmin, member of a group considered of highly intellectual and spiritually oriented people, with very strict discipline, that Ramanujan followed religiously even during his stay at Cambridge.

While meeting fellow mathematicians outside India, some

of them discovering our background of being Indians and Hindu, asked us about the so called caste system in India, and Ramanujan's exceptional characteristics, in particular of divinely qualities associated with his being a strict Brahmin. This further motivated us to write a book where we should explain in brief the caste system, the strict discipline followed by a Brahmin, and how Ramanujan, having been raised as a strict Brahmin had deep effect on his personality and in becoming a creative mathematician.

The book has been written for a common person having some interest in mathematics or in knowing about Ramanujan's life. It also contains matter on Ramanujan's life with perspectives of the Hindu-Brahmin divine phenomenon, he called 'goddess Namagiri,' in direct visualization of mathematical researches and wide support that he received from his teachers and community, including sympathetic and helpful treatment from the British who at that time were ruling India.

Ramanujan's life story and work has inspired numerous people and generations of mathematicians around the globe and continues to excite even today. We hope that this book will reach the current generation and generate interest in them to know more about Ramanujan's life and the areas influenced by him.

Readers will find photos, and letters written by Ramanujan and others containing his functioning and work on mathematics. Fortunately, a lot of this matter is available in the public domain from where we have accessed it. We greatly acknowledge and thank the various sources of this material, in particular the books [3], [4], [6], [9] and [13] mentioned in Section 14.2 of this book. Also, with the permission from the author and the publisher a copy of the article 'The SASTRA Ramanujan Prize: Its Origins and Its Winners', by Krishnaswami Alladi (see [2] in Section 14.3 of this book) has been attached in the appendix of this book, and we are extremely grateful to the publisher, American Mathematical Society, and the author Dr. Alladi for granting us the permission to do this.

Professor George E. Andrews, who is credited for finding the 'Lost Notebook of Ramanujan' is considered to be the world's foremost authority on Theory of Partitions, and on Ramanujan's work. He kindly wrote the Foreword to this book, and we are extremely grateful to him for all the time and effort that he has devoted in doing so.

Ritu Dhankhar of the Birla Institute of Technology and Science Pilani, India read the manuscript of this book and made many suggestions which considerably enhanced the quality of presentation in the book. We greatly appreciate all her interest and help in this regard.

We would like to thank Urmila Govil for her constant encouragement and support in writing this book. Also, our thanks are due to Avantha Kodithuwakku of the University of Kansas, Tagbo Aroh, Ziqin Feng, Dmitry Glotov, Stanley Spence and Jennifer Stone of the Department of Mathematics and Statistics, and Onyinye Rosemary Asogwa and Soundarya Korlapati of the Computer Science Department at Auburn University for their help in compiling and formatting some of the material in this book.

Finally, we express our deep appreciation to the Chairs T.Y. Tam, Ulrich Albrecht and Ash Abebe of the Department of Mathematics and Statistics, Auburn University for providing us with all the necessary support and encouragement during the period the book was written.

August 4, 2020

Narendra Kumar Govil
Bhu Dev Sharma

Contents

1

Birth, Home Town and Family

1.1 Introduction:

Ramanujan is known for his rich contributions in mathematics and no less for his strange, supernatural, mysterious ways of arriving at the quality and quantity of his researches in mathematics. He has inspired generations of mathematicians with his work and life story. His mentor, Professor G.H. Hardy compared him with other outstanding mathematicians of his time, giving him marks 100 out of 100 with no one equal or near equal to him. Ramanujan has been described as 'the *man who knew infinity,'* an inspired genius, a 'cosmos intuitionist' getting ideas and results at rather supreme consciousness level from infinite-knowledge reservoir through a divine source, he called *'Goddess Namagiri'.*

Higher State of Visualization

How did he reach that level? This is attributed to so many things that came to him from incidents in his life, unflinching practices, unabated spiritual thoughts, inspiration and upbringing. This all in his case, by closely following his life and what he himself solemnly attributed also had developed in the Hindu Vedic ways.

A brief suggestive attempt is made here to reflect on some of these factors. While in recorded mathematics history, he is a singular case of this happening, that too of a very high degree, there are scores of cases of clairvoyance, with ability to perceive matters beyond the range of ordinary perception. To an extent, to name some, Steve Jobs in the area of computer technology and Edgar Cayce in psychic-powers have shown these in USA. Perhaps Newton seeing the principle of gravitation in the falling of an apple and Archimedes shouting Eureka for having discovered the principle of liquid buoyancy while taking bath in bouquet show their sudden lapse in those states. These are examples of limited encounter with supreme Reality. Nobel Laureate in physics Erwin Schrödinger has of course, who wrote on Vedanta, has pointed out greater role of Vedic approach in shaping his thoughts. This kind of ancient Hindu state is recorded in some other cases also. It has been called, in Vedic-philosophical literature as the state of *Drishta*—'state of higher visualization'.

Some insight into Ramanujan's astonishing and surprising mathematical ways may as well be viewed in the Vedic system. In the Vedic philosophical system, knowledge is considered to be the infinite of the highest order. In totality it is called *vidya.* Vidya is further classified in two main categories—namely '*para-vidya*' and '*apara-vidya*'. Apara Vidya is knowledge assessable in conscious state from the outer wide world by different learning processes, scientific and other ways. Para-Vidya, on the other hand, is beyond apara-vidya—transfinite, accessible in meta-super-conscious state through what have been called the divine communications, that we have called 'cosmos intuitionism'.

Also, a very simple popular and deep philosophical concept is that of the 'third eye' that lets one perceive things far beyond the ordinary. A supernatural power, highly revered for bestowing this power, in Hindu metaphysical terms, is given the name *Lord Shiva.* A majority of the places of worship in India are shrines of *God Shiva.*

It may be briefly mentioned that Hindus fathomed philosophy for every world phenomena including numbers. They constructed a philosophy about numbers and their composition laws in the super conscious state. They applied mathematics to a vast world of astronomy. They developed their own calendar, in which all personal and social event records are kept. Astrologically, things are interpreted in terms of this calendar. This calendar has names of its months and dates *(tithies).* Time and location of the events are considered crucial for study of such records.

1.2 Birthday and Birth-town-Erode:

Ramanujan was born on ninth day of the Indian month of *Margasirsha* on Thursday, Dec. 22, 1887, just after the sunset. Place of birth was the house of his mother's parents in the town named *Erode* in Coimbatore district, a small town about 250 miles southwest of Madras (now Chennai). His mother was *Komalata-ammal* and father *Kuppuswamy Srinivasa Iyengar.* In those days, a woman giving birth to her first child at her parental house was a widely observed tradition there and so it was observed in Ramanujan's case as well.

Erode, located at the confluence of rivers *Cauvery* and *Bhavani,* had a population of about fifteen thousand people, when Ramanujan was born. River Cauvery is one of the seven most sacred rivers—*Ganga, Jamuna, Godavari, Saraswati, Narmada, Sindhu* and *Cauvery* in Indian subcontinent. Ganga, in the north being the most sacred, Cauvery is called the 'Ganga of South'. Not far from the river there was a little house that belonged to Komalata-ammal's father, a petty official in a lower court in Erode. Ramanujan was born in this house located on *Teppukulam Street* in the town's trading area which in those days was known as 'the fort'.

1.3 Name and the 'naming ceremony':

As per the Hindu-Vedic tradition, on eleventh day after the birth the '*Namkaran Sanskar*' was held in which the child was named 'Srinivasa Ramanujan Aiyangar'. In his name, 'Srinivasa' was in fact his father's name, and 'Aiyangar' referred to the particular branch of South Indian Brahmins to which he and his family belonged. Thus 'Ramanujan' was his given name, and he became known to the world by the name—'Ramanujan'.

Ramanujan's ancestral home in Kumbakonam

The town of Kumbakonam has its long history. Some thousand years back, it was the Capital of the Chola Empire. During the time of Ramanujan's birth, it had a population of little over 50,000 (now with a population of about 150,000). The town is bounded by two rivers, the *Cauvery River* to the north and *Arasalar River* to the south, and is located 40 kilometers from Thanjavur and 273 kilometers from Madras (now Chennai). It is the headquarters of the Kumbakonam 'taluk' of Thanjavur district.

Kumbakonam is known as a 'temple town' due to the prevalence of a number of temples here. It is one of India's sacred Hindu towns. The town is perhaps most well-known for its *Mahamaham* festival which is held every twelve lunar years when the Sun enters the constellation of Aquarius. It attracts people from all over the globe. In a ritual meant to absolve sins, pilgrims take bath in the *Mahamaham* tank, which symbolizes the waters of India's holy rivers.

It boasts of seventeen Hindu Temples. A majority of the temples are dedicated to honor the Hindu gods, Lord Vishnu and Lord Shiva. Twelve Shiva temples are connected with the Mahamaham festival. They are Kasi Viswanathar Temple, Kumbeswarar Temple, Nageswara Temple, Someswarar

Temple, Koteeswaran Temple, Kahahasteeswarar Temple, Gowthameswarar Temple, Amirthakalasanathar Temple, Banapuriswarar Temple, Abimukeswarar Temple, Kambatta Visvanathar Temple and Ekambareswarar Temple. Likewise, five Vishnu temples are connected with Mahamaham. They are Sarangapani Temple, Chakrapani Temple, Ramaswamy Temple, Rajagopalaswamy Temple, and Varahaperumal Temple. These grand temples are located in Kumbakonam.

Sarangapani Temple

The town, Kumbakonam's name is based on a legend, according to which here, after a deluge, the nectar of creation arrived in a sacred pot, which in Sanskrit is called *'Kumb'*. This sacred pot's nectar is believed to be in a pond. This legend has provided Kumbakonam a prime place in Hindu religious sacred places. It is considered as one of the five places where every 12 years, there is a massive festival, a congregation called Mahammakham in which around the pond of nectar, about a million people gather.

Sacredness and purity is attached to rivers and bath: In the traditional Hindu life, in contrast to wide practice where taking a regular bath is not a practice, everyone in India, in varying degrees of course, takes a daily bath early in the morning and observes a routine and values daily meditation time. Taking bath in a river is considered to be a sacred act that promotes intuition. Rivers, in India, vary in sacredness. A place of confluence of two or more rivers is called a *'Sangam'*. A sangam is considered to be very sacred. Staying and bathing there are ritualistic promptings that bring meritorious spiritual-mental advancement. The river Ganga, in north India is considered the most sacred of all rivers. The place of confluence of the rivers Ganga with Yamuna and the invisible Sarasvati, is considered to be the most celebrated Sangam in India. The river Cauvery is called River Ganga of South India and its banks are places for spiritual advancement.

Traditionally, four fairs are widely recognized as the Kumbh Melas: the Haridwar Kumbh Mela, the Prayagraj (Allahabad) Kumbh Mela, the Nashik-Trimbakeshwar Simhastha, and the Ujjain Simhastha. These four fairs are held periodically at one of the following places by rotation: Haridwar, Allahabad (now known as Prayagraj), Nashik district (Nashik and Trimbak), and Ujjain. The main festival site is located on the banks of a river: the Ganges (Ganga) at Haridwar; the confluence (Sangam) of the Ganges and the Yamuna and the invisible Sarasvati at Prayagraj (Allahabad); the Godavari at Nashik; and the Shipra at Ujjain. Bathing in these rivers is widely believed to cleanse a person of all sins.

Vedic routines of daily life: To essentially compose a person mentally away from distractions, great value is attached to—early rising, cleaning routine, regular bath preferably in a pious river, chanting of mantras, putting some holy marks from sandalwood paste, visit to a temple, inspirational reading and meditation are willingly accepted, because they result in conscious enhancement.

During the British rule, the town Kumbakonam where Ramanujan was being raised, was a prominent center of European education and Hindu culture. It acquired the cultural name, *'Cambridge of South India'*.

During the later part of the 20th century, the home in Kumbakonam where Ramanujan spent his childhood and produced more than 1000 theorems was in a dilapidated condition. This was, in spite of the fact that in India many events and conferences were organized in Ramanujan's memory, including the big conference organized in December 1987 on Ramanujan's Centenary celebrations. Unfortunately, nothing was done to preserve and renovate this historic home of Ramanujan, which was very much needed in order to honor and preserve the legacy of Ramanujan.

This town of Kumbakonam has in recent years come to prominence with the establishment of the Shanmugha Arts, Science, Technology and Research Academy (more popularly known as SASTRA University). This university which was established as Shanmugha College of Engineering in 1984 at Thanjavur (now known as Tanjore) of which Kumbakonam is a Taluk, is a private institution. Since the establishment, it has now grown by leaps and bounds and has been attracting some of the brightest students and faculty, both from India and abroad.

It was in 2003, that SASTRA University purchased the historic home of Ramanujan, decorated it beautifully and converted it into a museum. In this museum are displayed several important letters, photographs and documents related to Ramanujan. In order to maintain the originality of this historic home, no changes in the structure or design have been made, except adding a bust of Ramanujan in the living room.

In December 2003, to mark this occasion of purchasing Ramanujan's home, the SASTRA University organized an International Conference on *'Number Theory for Secure Communications,'* at Kumbakonam campus from December 20 to December 22, 2003. The conference coincided with 116th Birth Anniversary of Srinivasa Ramanujan, whose work on Number theory made India proud. Dr. A.P.J. Abdul Kalam, the then President of India, came on December 20, 2003 to inaugurate this conference. He declared Ramanujan's home, where Ramanujan had stayed for over 15 years and generated more than 1000 theorems, before leaving for Trinity College, England as a national treasure and an International Monument, because it is in this house that the vibrations of the thoughts of Ramanujan are being felt and will formally admitted in a local school (called *paathshala)* with the chants of Vedic Mantras.

Though as it shows later, he was a brilliant child, but Ramanujan did not like going to school. His approach to learning can perhaps be called contemplative rather than bookish. This highlights his being a very differently orientated individual, not much by tutoring but instead of his own pursuit, that perhaps accounts for his totally untutored research in mathematics.

For family reasons, for three years, he spent time for small periods of time in Kumbakonam, Kanchipuram and Madras (now Chennai). In Kanchipuram, the medium of his education was Telugu. In later part of 1895, he was a student at Kangayan Primary School in Kumbakonam. Though it was not normal in India those years to introduce English as a subject that early stage of life, however in that school he learnt English well from his early years.

At the age of 9, he had primary level examinations in English, Tamil, Mathematics, and Geography etc. and topped these exams in the whole district. Thereafter he joined Town High School, where mostly bright students were admitted. In his time, the principal of this school, Mr. Krishnaswami Iyer, was a strict disciplinarian. Slowly, Ramanujan came to be recognized for his brightness. His classmates started flocking around him for help in Mathematics. In third year of the school he started asking his teachers tough questions.

2.2 Spirit and pride for excellence in mathematics:

It may be noted that right from school time, Mathematics was not only a subject of his interest but as well an area of taking pride by showing his talent and excellence in it. He wanted to be second to none in the subject. At the age of nine, in the examination of Primary level, in mathematics he scored 42 out of 45, while another student named Sarangapani scored 43. Ramanujan was greatly hurt by this in spite of Sarangapani telling him that he has done far better in other subjects.

2.3 Meeting seniors, studying advanced books and asking questions:

Another feature that we find is the sympathy, support and appreciation he received from persons who came in his touch. He also got the opportunity to interact with students of higher classes in studies.

In order to improve the financial situation, his family used to keep some students as paying guests in their house. Two students, one from Trichinopoly and the other from Tirunelveli, of the Government College were staying in his house. From them, he learnt mathematics of the graduate level, and could comfortably discuss and help them in solving their problems.

While he was about the age of 11, he started asking more unusual questions and attempting his own ways of solving simple problems, and also studying books of higher classes. Since two students of higher classes were staying in his house as paying guests, he requested them to bring some advanced level books from their library. Among the books he received was the book *'Plane Trigonometry'* by S.L. Loney, published in Cambridge, England in 1894. The book in fact contains many more topics other than trigonometry, like exponential function, logarithm of a complex number, calculation of pi, hyperbolic functions, infinite products, Gregory series and infinite series. Series expansion of some trigonometric functions is also given in this book. Part II of the book has chapters on advanced topics. Ramanujan, by the age of 13 years mastered all these. He learnt trigonometric functions not only in terms of ratios of sides of a right triangle, but also as a infinite series.

Although Ramanujan had mastered this book, but it was the book of Carr (discussed below) that triggered Ramanujan's curiosity.

2.4 The book that triggered Ramanujan:

In 1903, when he was 16, while interacting with a senior friendly person, who knew his interest and skills in mathematics, brought to him from the library a copy of the book *A Synopsis of Elementary Results in Pure and Applied Mathematics,* written by a tutor named George Shoobridge Carr. The book was primarily meant to help students cram the results and prepare for examinations.

Young Ramanujan's dialogue with the 'Elderly friend', who brought the book, as recorded by one of his early biographer, Ranganathan, is as follows:

Ramanujan: What is this big book about?

Elderly friend: I am showing it to you purposely.

Ramanujan: What is it, uncle?

Elderly friend: Did you not master Loney's Trigonometry when you were 12? Are you not the boy who has calculated the length of equator of the earth?

Ramanujan: You are pulling my leg, uncle. Do not mention that. Please tell me about this book.

Elderly friend: This is the book *'A Synopsis of Elementary Results in Pure and Applied Mathematics'*, by George Shoobridge Carr.

Ramanujan: Will you please allow me to glance through the book? (Turning pages of the book and looking at these, said)....... They are all very interesting!

Elderly friend: I am glad you like it. Keep it with you for some time.

Ramanujan: Grateful, uncle.

This book belonged to the library of the Government College in Kumbakonam, but was later published with a different title. The book served the purpose of providing a big bunch of mathematical problems without solutions. It triggered Ramanujan. He got problems to solve and create fresh problems obtaining concrete results and their generalizations.

It may be remarked that Carr was a tutor at Cambridge and his this book carried a collection of about 5000 theorems, with no solutions or methods for that, with occasional minor hints of some. Ramanujan set out to prove all these formulas anew and also to obtain their generalizations. For this, sometimes he invented his own notations. Here it may as well be mentioned that Ramanujan never learned about functions of complex variable, but made profound contributions to the fields of elliptic and modular functions, which were discovered by ancient Indian mathematician Madhava in the fourteenth century and were rediscovered by Newton and Leibnitz in the seventeenth century.

This book, 'Synopsis of Elementary Results in Pure and Applied Mathematics' (in short 'Synopsis') by George Shoobridge Carr was published in 1886. It may be noted that Carr had prepared this book for persons preparing for a rather prestigious and challenging examination, 'Tripos', the examination in which success was very rewarding in making a good career. As mentioned above, the book contained around five thousand mathematical theorems, propositions, diagrams, formulas, statements, etc. unlike Loney's Trigonometry, with practically no proofs. It has short hints only for few, but no clue of directions for the students preparing for 'Tripos'. Unfortunately, this book is not widely available now except in some prestigious libraries, like that of Cambridge University.

Richard Askey, who had access to the book, has written that in every chapter of Synopsis, formulas and propositions have serially been written. In the book some numbers are skipped. His guess is that perhaps the author had in his mind to put there some definite material in future. In all, some 1300 places are empty, the book contains exactly 4865 number of formulas in the areas of algebra, trigonometry, analytical geometry, and calculus.

2.5 Ramanujan Maintaining Notebooks:

Ramanujan used to perform all the calculations on a slate because he could not afford paper for this purpose. By working mathematical details on a slate and after having reached the stage of good formulation, he fortunately, entered the final results in brief on a register—the *'Note Book'.* These note books contain the treasures of Ramanujan's mathematics, and mathematicians have been mining these treasures. An immediate purpose of maintaining these registers may perhaps have been that in bad time, he could show and impress the prospective employer when looking for a job. Ramanujan's first Notebook was on hypergeometric series, continued fractions, singular moduli and some aspects of number theory. It has chapters and theorems numbered consecutively.

To have some more idea of these notebooks, it may be noted, that the things recorded there were by Ramanujan for himself not for others. These were, in general not in notations in current mathematical professional circles. He coined his own notations. Formulations of problems and their applications or examples were not used in general to explain the ideas for the readers. It was the work what may be called 'pure' mathematics.

For example, consider the equation $x^2 + 7 = 2^n$, and determine, for integer values of *n,* and corresponding integer values of *x* that satisfy the equation. One can immediately say that equation is satisfied "for $n = 3$, giving $x = 1$, these together being provide integer solution of the given equation. Trying a little more for $n = 4, 5, 7, 1\ 5$, one gets corresponding values of $x = 3,5,11,181$". Trying harder and harder, one does not get any other solution. It was the genius of Ramanujan to profess that these are the only five integer solutions for this equation. It was in 1948 that Tyrgve Nagell proved it so. How did Ramanujan conjecture it? He did not give any proof. His intuition, what else! Perhaps his answer would have been the 'goddess Namagiri'.

In mathematics, a result is not accepted unless it is flawlessly proved in clear terms. Also, mathematics grows by the process of generalizing results proved earlier for a particular case. This leads to research and the process has greatly widened the ambit of mathematics. It is believed that Ramanujan had started writing proofs of the results and their generalizations stated in Carr's book in 1904, in the registers later to be called his *'Notebooks'.* He wrote with green colored ink. According to Prof G.N. Watson, before going to England, the number of results that Ramanujan had in these notebooks was somewhere between 3000 and 4000.

2.6 At school:

During this early period, he learnt the method of solving cubic equations, from one of the seniors. In Trigonometry also, he was not confined to definitions of trigonometric functions like sine, cosine of an angle as ratios of sides of a right-angled triangle, but knew their infinite series expansions. In 1903, he passed class X exam from Madras University. Later in 1904, when he was awarded the *'Ranganatha Rao Prize'*, Principal Mr. Krishnaswami Iyer praised Ramanujan by the remark that "his school results do not quite reflect his ability. He is far ahead of the total marks assigned to him in the exam".

After High School Examination with highest marks in English and Mathematics, Ramanujan got *'Subrahmanyam Scholarship'*, and entered the Government College in Kumbakonam for further education.

As a student in class XI, Ramanujan started remaining absorbed all the time in mathematics neglecting other subjects—English, History, etc. His research in mathematics continued rather quietly. Of course, he did show his several results on infinite series, that he had discovered himself to his mathematics teacher, Mr. Seshu Aiyar, who greatly appreciated them and advised Ramanujan to also pay attention to other subjects.

Ramanujan could not apply himself in any subject other than mathematics. In fact, he did not study any subject in which things were only to be memorized. It is mentioned that his analytical mind had no interesting psychology, in which diagrams were used to be made. As a consequence, except in Mathematics, he predictably failed in all the subjects at annual XI class examination. This resulted in his failure to go to class XII and loss of scholarship.

His mother was very confident of him and so was very angry on school authorities for Ramanujan's failure and loss of scholarship. Kumbakonam being a town of lawyers, she went to several lawyers and prepared a petition. She met the Principal of the school and put forth the argument requesting special consideration for Ramanujan for his exceptional mathematical skills. The Principal was unable to do that.

After leaving school for a period of five years he was neither a student, nor on any job. He was not in touch with a teacher or researcher as well. He had no resources for any of that. But his creative work in mathematics continued unabated. Instead of seeking a job, he started tutoring students. His income from tuitions was at the best Indian Rupees 5.00 per month. Parents, relatives and friends were well aware of his talents, interests and pursuits. He had full freedom and unflinching support for doing mathematics. He would spend long hours unmindfully sitting on floor holding slate in hand writing and erasing things on it.

About a year after Ramanujan dropped out of the school, he independently developed and investigated the Bernoulli numbers and calculated the Euler-Mascheroni constant up to 15 decimal places. His peers at the time commented that they 'rarely understood him' and 'stood in respectful awe' of him.

2.7 A School Dropout:

Losing the scholarship was a great setback to Ramanujan. Beside shame and public disgrace, it meant financial problems. His poor father made just as much as was his tuition fee in the college and the family therefore could not afford his continuing in the college, but he needed it to continue further. To improve the financial condition, he made efforts to earn by tutoring students, and by working on accounts-keeping of some businesses. He did get some students for coaching in mathematics, but while teaching, he unmindfully used to switch to explaining things and material that were not in course, rather were confusing to the students, and so this also did not work.

Mindful of the financial position of his father, with a view to be a helpful member, he decided to take up some regular employment. At the suggestion of a friend, in search of a suitable job, he even went to Vishakhapatnam (near Vijayawada) without informing his parents. There he stayed in a temple. His parents were greatly upset and made attempts to search him. His mother found out that he was in Vishakhapatnam and went all the way to bring him back. She hid herself behind the temple door and when he came back after his bath, she confronted him and brought him back home. The parents some how managed to his late admission in the college. However, for short attendances, he could not appear in class XI examination in 1905.

A year after his above failure in Kumbakonam, in 1906 Ramanujan came to stay with his grandmother in Chennai to give a try there for further education at Pachaiyappa's College.

According to his grandmother, Ramanujan, even when he was a child, had the habit of lying down and working with numbers for long hours. He would scribble all kinds of calculations on any sheet of paper that he could lay his hands on. If someone would knock at his door, he would never open it. He would simply peep out of his window and tell the visitor that no one was home, and promptly will be back to his calculations.

Mr. N. Ramanujachariar, his new mathematics teacher, being greatly impressed by Ramanujan's Notebook took him to the principal, who awarded Ramanujan, a small scholarship. At Pachaiyappa's College, again at the end of the first year itself he failed all the examinations. This happened because, although a gifted mathematician, he did not clear in other subjects.

Thereafter, in 1907, he privately took Class XII examination and failed again. With this unfortunately his formal student period ended. Notwithstanding these setbacks, his mathematical pursuits continued unabated, and rather accelerated.

2.8 Beginning Research:

Ramanujan's research may be considered to have begun right from his early childhood. His was an inquisitive mind. He had questions for everything, not just in mathematics: like why water evaporates when put over the oven? How to measure distances between clouds?

There is an incident of early childhood to give an idea of such a functioning of his mind. Explaining the concept of division, once his mathematics teacher said in the class, "If three bananas are distributed to three children, every child will get one banana," and he went on to its simple generalization. On this Ramanujan raised a question, "If zero bananas are distributed to zero number of students, will then also each child will receive one banana?" This obviously is the problem of dividing zero by zero, and the correct answer in mathematics is 'indeterminate'. In his mind what may be called mythical ways of studying numbers had taken roots quite early in life.

Mathematical studies, as is common knowledge, have to deal with numbers, constants, variables, functions, and equations etc. He understood and remembered topicalities'of various kinds of numbers—natural numbers, real numbers, rational numbers, irrational numbers, algebraic numbers, prime numbers, composite numbers, and several other classes. Mathematics students coming to secondary school should be on friendly terms with numbers. They need to know at least some of the many relationships between them. Perfect squares are quick to recognize. Numbers that are one less than a perfect square are the product of two whole numbers which differ by 2, like:

16-1 = 15 = 3 x 5, 9-1 = 8 = 2 x 4, 36-1 = 35 = 5 x 7, etc.

While numbers are constants, there are special and important other constant numbers like π(pi) and *'e'*, and right from early age, Ramanujan's mind started spending time in the thick 'garden of numbers'.

It is believed that he had independently obtained series expansion for e, which was known to mathematics from Euler's time. While Ramanujan, was still at high school, he discovered that $e^{\pi i} + 1 = 0$, a surprising equality result between e,π,*i*,*0*, and 1. He was, in fact greatly disappointed to learn later that Euler had found the same result in 1743. (refer David Wells: You are a Mathematician, PENGUIN BOOKS, page 312).

Ramanujan's such intriguing and surprisingly attractive results have greatly inspired people to develop interest in mathematics. The centenary of Ramanujan's birth was celebrated by a conference at which the celebrated physicist Freeman Dyson contributed a paper titled *'A Walk through Ramanujan's Garden'*, which he concluded by:

"The collected papers of Ramanujan have traveled with me from England to America and are still as fresh to-day as they were in 1940. Whenever I am angry or depressed, I pull down Ramanujan's collected papers from the shelf and take a quite stroll in Ramanujan's garden. I recommend this therapy to all of you who suffer from headaches or jangled nerves. And Ramanujan's papers are not only a good therapy for headaches, they also are full of beautiful ideas which may help you to do more interesting mathematics".

□

3

Marriage and Search for A Job

For about six years after leaving the school, Ramanujan's life was not normal. He had become a matter of concern for the family. Unemployed, under financial difficulties, outside the school, away from all worldly turmoil he could be seen sitting with slate and chalk working on mathematics. At the age of 20, his parents planned to get him married, thinking that this might be the solution for his odd life pattern. In India, putting the burden of marriage, particularly in those days, was considered the way out to grow a young man and to put him on even road of life. Also, Indian marriages, in general are arranged, under strict restrictions of age, caste, sub-caste, family, astrological compatibility, etc. The search for the spouse, considered primarily as the responsibility of the parents, undergoes through relatives and acquaints by reference and in-betweens.

3.1 Mother arranged the marriage:

One day in 1908, when Ramaunujan's mother was visiting a family-friend in Rajendram, a village located at a distance of about 80 miles west of Kumbakonam, she learnt of a bright-eyed girl, Janaki, daughter of a distant relative, who was a very unassuming and pretty girl. Ramanujan's mother believed in the matching of horoscopes for marriage, and she herself being an astrologer could see if the horoscopes of Ramanujan and Janaki matched. She therefore asked for the horoscope of Janaki, which was provided to her. She drew the horoscope of Ramanujan on a wall of the house and finding his horoscope matching with that of Janaki, she

3.2 Search for a job:

In 1910, by securing money from some of his friends, Ramanujan went to Madras (now named Chennai) in search of a job, and over there, for some time, he stayed with Mr. Viswanatha Sastri in Victoria Student Hostel, a large red and black brick structure near the Presidency College. Viswanatha Sastri was studying at Presidency College and to him Ramanujan had tutored earlier.

In Madras (now Chennai), early in the morning, he would go out in search of tuitions. He enjoyed tutoring Mathematics to students but his reputation of not sticking to the course material caused him problems. One day, he would teach student using the standard method but in case the student forgot this method and asked him again then next day he will improvise to entirely new method in order to teach the subject, which the student's regular teacher would never have touched in the class. This made things very difficult for the student to understand. For example, Viswanatha in his memoirs has narrated that with such disappointing responses, Ramanujan sometimes at night will curse his fate and will become very sad. Then, Sastri will console him by saying that his brilliant command on mathematics will be a boom one day. On this Ramanujan will utter, "Just as Galileo etc. died in inquisition, same way without getting any recognition, I will also perish one day".

Later in 1910 itself, at the invitation of an old friend, Mr. K. Narasimha Iyengar, and his brother Sarangapani of Kumbakonam, Ramanujan moved to Venkat Lane in 'Park Town'. Narasimha was studying in Madras Christian College and Ramanujan used to help him in mathematics.

Unfortunately, due to lack of enough education, and not having a degree, Ramanujan did not succeed in getting a regular job. He became unwell and moved to the place of his old classmate Radhakrishan Iyyer, who was rather shocked to see Ramanujan's health and illness. He took him to see a doctor. Doctor advised Ramanujan to go back home to Kumbakonam and live with his family.

Ramanujan, because of being ill, had lost his self-confidence.

When leaving for Kumbakonam by train, he took out his two Notebooks which had his theorems and results mentioned therein. Handing these over to Radhakrishnan he said, "If I die, then please hand over these Notebooks either to Mathematics Professor Singaravelu Mudaliar or to Professor Edward B. Ross of Madras Christian College".

After staying home at Kumbakonam, he recovered from illness. Thereafter, in search of a job, he again went to Madras (now Chennai). This time he changed his search concerning employment, by deciding to look for employment in offices rather than for the tuitions. He decided to meet some influential persons. While meeting such people he carried his Notebooks along. The Notebooks had become his great assets, and rather served as letter of recommendation for this purpose.

3.3 Meeting Mr. Ramaswamy Iyer:

He decided to meet Mr. Ramaswamy Iyer, a Deputy Collector. One day, on his way to Pandicherry, he changed train at Villupuram and reached at Tirukoilur to meet him.

Though Mr. Iyer was not teaching in a university or college, yet people used to address him as 'Professor'. He had special interest in geometry and during his student life at Presidency College he had sent an article on Mathematics for publication in 'Educational Times', published from England. Sometime earlier, he also had an active role in the establishment of 'Indian Mathematical Society', and was thus one of the founders of the Indian Mathematical Society.

Ramanujan met Ramaswamy Iyer. The only recommendation that Ramanujan had was his Notebooks, which by then contained several results on Magic Squares, Prime Numbers, Infinite Series, Divergent Series, Partitions, Continued Fractions, Bernoulli Numbers, Riemann Zeta Function, Hypergeometric Series, Elliptic Functions, Modular Equations, etc. and asked for a clerical job in his office.

Ramaswamy Iyer perhaps did not follow much in the Notebooks, but was still quite impressed. He could easily offer Ramanujan a job in Taxes-office. However, in his memoirs, he has written that he did not do so because by doing so, he would have spoiled the future chances of Ramanujan's talent. Mr. Iyer later recalled: "I was struck by the extraordinary mathematical results contained in the notebooks. I had no mind to smother his genius by an appointment in the lowest rungs of the revenue department". Fortunately, a brief account of what went on in the interview, (see Bhavans Journal, July 1, 1987, pp. 30-31) is available. It is given below.

Ramanujan—I am interested in Mathematics.

Ramaswamy Iyer—Is it so? Come along. Kindly take your seat. What have you done so far?

Ramanujan—This Notebook contains some of the theorems and results obtained by me.

Ramaswamy Iyer—Pass it on to me. Most of these appear to be new. My goodness! Whatever page I look into, I find it to be a mine of new theorems and formulae. What a feast! Where are you working?

Ramanujan—I am unemployed.

Ramaswamy Iyer—(Still turning the pages of the Notebook) I hope you have sufficient ancestral property.

Ramanujan—No, Sir, my family is poor. My father is a petty clerk in a cloth merchant's shop in Kumbakonam. Moreover, Sir, last year my parents made me enter into married life.

Ramaswamy Iyer—(still with his hand buried in the Notebook) Is it so?

Ramanujan—Sir, be pleased to give me a clerk's post either in your office or in the Taluka's Board office. I can then earn my livelihood.

Ramaswamy Iyer—It is too bad. If you become a clerk in any of these offices, your mathematical abilities will soon disappear. I do not want to sin that way.

Ramanujan—Sir, you should not say like that. Who else will help me?

Ramaswamy Iyer—Do not think that I want to disappoint you. You will get some real help. Just wait for few minutes. (Then Ramaswamy went into his office room and wrote a letter of recommendation to P.V. Seshu Aiyar, Professor of Mathematics at the Presidency College, Madras (now Chennai).

Ramaswamy Iyer—Take this letter, Ramanujan, go and meet Professor Seshu Aiyar and give him this letter. Do you know him at all?

Ramanujan—Yes, Sir. I was his student in the Government College, Kumbakonam.

Ramaswamy Iyer—Then it will be easy for you to meet him.

Accordingly, Ramanujan now left for Madras (now Chennai) and met Seshu Aiyar who by that time had moved to Presidency College, Madras (now Chennai). Ramanujan had his notebooks in his hand, and a letter of recommendation from Professor Ramaswamy Iyer. It appears that Seshu Aiyar had lot of sympathy towards Ramanujan but in spite of his best efforts he could not arrange any job or scholarship for Ramanujan to study Mathematics. It is speculated that Seshu Aiyar supplied Ramanujan with a letter of introduction for Mr. R. Ramachandra Rao.

Mr. Ramachandra Rao was the District Collector of Nellore, a town with a population of about 35,000 and located about 100 miles from Madras (now Chennai). Mr. Rao was a very bright person, belonged to a very rich family, and got an education at the Presidency College, Madras (now Chennai). At the young age of nineteen years, he joined the Provincial Civil Service. Besides, he was also known as a mathematician and had been serving as the Secretary of the Indian Mathematical Society.

Although, Ramanujan had a letter of introduction for Ramachandra Rao but he was not bold enough to meet Ramachandra Rao. Instead of going to Nellore, he decided to go back to his home in Kumbakonam. While in Madras (now Chennai), he met one of his old friends named Rajagopalachari. Rajagopalachari was just few months older than Ramanujan, grown up in the same town as Ramanujan, used to go to the same temple as Ramanujan and even attended the same Town High School with him. Ramanujan and Rajagopalachari had lost contact of each other for about a decade and when Ramanujan told him the story of his failure and that after making all the unsuccessful efforts to get a job he is going back to Kumbakonam, Rajagopalachari advised him not to go home and instead meet Ramachandra Rao, a powerful person. He gave Ramanujan the needed push in order to meet Mr. Rao. He even offered to accompany Ramanujan while he goes to see Mr. Rao. Also, he agreed to bear the expenses that Ramanujan will have to incur in order to stay for few extra days in Madras (now Chennai). Ramanujan then canceled his plan of going to Kumbakonam and instead decided to take his chance to meet Mr. Rao.

It turned out that Ramachandra Rao had a nephew who happened to know Ramanujan. It was, in fact, he who helped in arranging the meeting of Ramanujan and his friend Rajagopalachari with his uncle Ramachandra Rao.

Ramanujan and his friend Rajagopalachari met Mr. Rao four times to convince him about the abilities and extra ordinary talent of Ramanujan. In the first three meetings, Rao was impressed by Ramanujan's research but was not sure if it was his work, and so declined any help in getting him a job. In the fourth meeting Ramanujan and his friend Rajagopalachari went to see Ramachandra Rao with correspondence that Ramanujan had with Professor Saldhana, an eminent Indian mathematician from Bombay (now Mumbai) to whom Ramanujan had sent some of his theorems. Although Saldhana's letter expressed lack of understanding of Ramanujan's work but concluded that he was not a fony person and the work was genuine. Ramanujan's friend Rajagopalachari who was accompanying Ramanujan also tried to remove any doubts that Rao had about Ramanujan's integrity. Thus, after looking at Saldhana's letter and listening to Rajagopalachari, Ramachandra Rao got interested in Ramanujan's work and asked him to explain some of his more accessible results, which he could understand. On this, Ramanujan led him step-by-step to Elliptic Integrals and Hypergeometric Series and at last to his Theory of Divergent Series. Ramachandra Rao started to feel that Ramanujan's work was indeed genuine and that it must be examined by eminent mathematicians. When Ramachandra Rao asked what kind of help does he need, Ramanujan simply replied that he wants a job by which he has financial assistance to have simple food without much exertion, so that he may fully devote himself to do research in Mathematics.

Ramachandra Rao told him that he will not like to give him a job in Nellore because he thought it will be cruel to make an intellectual giant like Ramanujan rot in a place like Nellore.

He instead sent him back to Seshu Aiyar with a letter telling him that in spite of his failing examinations Seshu Aiyar would arrange Ramanujan a scholarship by which he will be able to live comfortably and continue doing research in Mathematics. Ramanujan then went back to Seshu Aiyar in Madras (now Chennai) and from then (sometimes from early 1911) he started receiving twenty-five rupees per month by money order from Ramachandra Rao. This provided Ramanujan with all that he needed in order to devote himself continue doing his research in Mathematics. Many people, in India and England felt proud that they had helped Ramanujan, but of them all, perhaps Ramachandra Rao was the one who deserves highest praise.

3.4 His first research publication on Bernoulli Numbers:

Even, during all this period when Ramanujan had been trying to secure an employment, he did not slacken in doing his research work in Mathematics. His first contribution to the *Journal of the Indian Mathematical Society* was in the form of questions communicated by Seshu Aiyar and appeared in February issue of this journal. His long paper, titled *'Some Properties of Bernoulli Numbers'* appeared in the *Journal of the Indian Mathematical Society* 3 (1911), 219-234. In this paper, Ramanujan found connections between things that really did not seem to be connected. The paper had eight theorems, containing arithmetical properties of Bernoulli numbers, and provided proofs of three of them. The proofs provided in the paper were either only sketchy or sometimes even incomplete, but still the paper attracted considerable attention from the readers and provided them many entertaining problems to work on.

One of the first problems he posed as Question 289, in the journal was to ask the readers to evaluate:

$$\sqrt{1+2\sqrt{1+3\sqrt{1+\cdots}}}$$

which seemed to be straightforward arithmetic, with no *x* or *y* to complicate it. He waited for a solution to be offered in three issues but failed to receive any solution. At last, Ramanujan supplied the solution to the problem by himself. He supplied the following more general equation from the Page 105 of his notebook.

$$x+n+a=\sqrt{ax+(n+a)^2+x\sqrt{a(x+n)+(n+a)^2+(x+n)\sqrt{\cdots}}}$$

The above equation could be used to solve infinitely many nested radicals problems. In the above equation if we set x=2, n=1, and a=0, one gets the answer to the question posed in the journal as simply 3.

Also, this paper helped Ramanujan becoming known to the mathematical community as a mathematician. In 1912, he published two more notes *"On Q. 330 of Prof Sanjana,* 4 (1912), 59-61" and *"A set of equations,* 4 (1912), 94-96", in the fourth volume of the same journal, where he raised several questions asking for solutions. Although, Ramanujan's methods were so much tense and novel, but due to the lack of training his presentations were lacking in clarity and precision as well. As a result, it was difficult to follow things for an ordinary reader who is not used to such intellectual gymnastics.

It may be remarked that Ramanujan did not use paper to do his research, and instead he always worked on a big slate, which is still preserved with the family of S. Narayana Iyer. When Ramanujan was leaving for England, S. Narayana Iyer traded his slate with that of Ramanujan, so that the same could be preserved. In this regard, he once told his friend K.S. Srinivasan that if he worked Mathematics on paper then he would need four reams of it, which he could not afford. For this reason, he was working on the slate and was using his elbow to erase, which had made his elbow rough, dirty and black.

3.5 Job of a clerk at Madras Port Trust:

For about a year Ramanujan lived on Ramachandra Rao's generosity. He had been sending him twenty-five rupees per month. During this period, he had been very productive in his work and was completing his second paper with many interesting results and problems. In spite of all this, he did not appear to be comfortable because of him being a possible burden on Ramachandra Rao and so was interested in getting a regular job so that he is no more a burden on Ramachandra Rao and also may plan his life and bring his family to Madras (now Chennai). From January 12 to February 21, 1912, he even worked on a temporary job in the office of the Accountant General, Madras (now Chennai) on pay of twenty Indian rupees per month, but then on 9th February 1912 at the suggestion of Ramachandra Rao he applied for the position of a clerk in the office of Chief Accountant, Madras Port Trust. The Madras Port Trust carried over 60 percent of the imports and exports of Madras presidency to Britain. The letter he wrote is given below, and also accompanied to his application was a recommendation letter from E.W. Middlemast, a Mathematics Professor at the Presidency College, Madras (now Chennai) who wrote that Ramanujan was, "a young man of quite exceptional capacity in Mathematics".

Ramachandra Rao

9 February, 1912
Triplecane

S. Ramanujan
7 Summer House
Triplecane

To
The Chief Accountant
Port Trust, Madras

Sir,
I understand there is a clerkship vacant in your office, and I beg to apply for the same. I have passed the Matriculation Examination and studied up to the F.A. but was prevented from pursuing my studies owing to several untoward circumstances. I have, however been devoting all my time to Mathematics and developing the subject. I can say I am quite confident I can do justice to my work if I am appointed to the post. I therefore beg to request that you will be good enough to confer the appointment to me.

I beg to remain, Sir

Your most obedient Servant
S. *Ramanujan*

The Chairman of the Madras Port Trust those days was Sir Francis Joseph Edward Spring, who played a pioneering role in the development of the Indian Railways. He was born on 20th January 1849 in Baltimore, Cork County in Ireland, and studied at Trinity College, Cambridge. After graduating from there in 1870, he joined the engineering section of the Indian Imperial Civil Service, where he served as Consulting Engineer to the Government of India. Besides his many other achievements he was credited with the construction of a big railroad bridge across the Godavari River. After retiring from the civil service in 1904, he was appointed Chairman of the Madras Port Trust. He served in that capacity until 1919, where he redesigned and modernized the harbor at Madras both by increasing its capacity and improving its defenses against cyclones. He was a fellow of the University of Madras and of the University of Calcutta, and throughout his career he had been publishing in engineering and India-focused journals.

On 1st March 1912, just about three weeks after Ramanujan had applied for a job at the Madras Port Trust, Ramanujan came to know that he has been appointed as a Class III, Grade IV clerk in the accounts section of the Madras Port Trust at a pay of thirty rupees per month. It is believed that he got this job on the recommendation of Ramachandra Rao. Also, Ramachandra Rao wrote to Professor C.L. Griffith of the Engineering College, Madras (now Chennai) requesting him to inform Sir Francis Spring about the mathematical talent of Ramanujan.

Professor C.L. Griffith, whose full name was Charles Leopold Troyte Griffith, was born on 6th June 1872 and had received his scientific training at the University College, London from 1890 to 1892. He was an Associate Member of the Institute of Civil Engineers and Professor of Civil Engineering at the Madras College of Engineering.

At the recommendation of B. Ramachandra Rao, on 12 November 1912, Professor Griffith wrote to Sir Francis Spring the following letter.

College of Engineering
Madras

Dear Sir Francis,

You have in your office as an accountant on thirty rupees per month, a young man named S. Ramanujan who is a most remarkable mathematician. He may be very poor accountant, but I hope you will see that he is kept happily employed until something can be done to make use of his extraordinary gifts. I am writing to one of the leading mathematical professors at home about him and sending copies of some of Ramanujan's papers and results. Our Math. Professor here says that very few people could follow or criticize the work. It is of course far beyond my scope, but I happen to know who is at work in the same line at home, and I hope to get instructions as to what this fellow ought to do.

If there is any real genius in him he will have to be provided with money for books and with leisure, but until I hear from home, I don't feel sure that it is worthwhile spending much time or money on him.

Yours sincerely,

C.L.T. Griffith

Besides, Ramachandra Rao had also given Sir Francis Spring the information about Ramanujan's talent and interest in Mathematics and thus Sir Francis Spring knew what kind of clerk he was getting. This helped Ramanujan to receive all possible assistance needed for him to continue working in Mathematics, while being on the job as a clerk at Madras Port Trust.

At Madras Port Trust Ramanujan's immediate superior was S. Narayana Iyer, who was the Chief Accountant. S. Narayana Iyer was born on 15th December 1874 in Cumbum, near Madurai, Tamil Nadu, as mentioned earlier, a state in the southern part of India. He had one elder brother and one sister. His father was Subbanarayana Iyer and mother Lakshmi, and they were very poor. His father came from a family of astrologers and was an honorary astrologer at the Goddess Meenakshi temple in Madurai. Being a Hindu priest, he was quite good in Sanskrit and Vedas. He earned his living by conducting Hindu rituals in private homes. Because of Narayana Iyer being raised up in a poor family he had developed concern and affection towards poor and for everyone he worked with. In 1896, Narayana Iyer received his M.A. in Mathematics from St. Joseph's College, in Trichinopoly and soon became a lecturer in Mathematics there. There he met Sir Francis Spring who at that time was also in Trichinopoly serving in the Railways Golden Rock Workshop. Sometime in 1900, Narayana Iyer left St. Joseph's College and joined the Public Works Department in Madras (now Chennai). By then, Sir Francis Spring had become Chairman of the Madras Port Trust, and asked Narayana Iyer to join Madras Port Trust as Office Manager, which he did. But by the time in February 1912, Ramanujan applied for a clerk's job in Madras Port Trust, Narayana Iyer had been promoted to Chief Accountant, and was the highest ranking Indian at the port trust. Over there, he worked on this position till his retirement in 1934. He did not take good care of his health and died on 17th January 1937 at the age of about 63 years. He was scrupulously honest, religious and was greatly influenced by the great spiritual saint Ramana Maharishi in Tiruvannamalai. He was very simple and although he could have easily afforded to travel by a more comfortable transport but he always traveled to and from work by tramcar, the transport meant for common people.

Those days for Indians, the boots and trousers with the European coat constituted the most convenient dress for moving about quickly, but in spite of this Narayana Iyer never gave away to Western dress and instead wore the traditional *dhoti* and *turban* all his life.

In recognition of his services, he was awarded, by the Government, the title of 'Rao Bahadur', a title of respect awarded to important people during the reign of the British Empire in India. In 1907, he became a founding member of the Indian Mathematical Club, which soon in 1909 became the Indian Mathematical Society. He served as the Club's first Assistant Secretary from 1907 to 1910, and later during 1914-1928, its Treasurer. He published two papers in the Journal of the Indian Mathematical Society, outlining some of the discoveries of Ramanujan in the Theory of Prime Numbers, and some applications of his 'Master theorem' for evaluation of integrals.

At the office, Ramanujan's job included verifying accounts and establishing cash balances which was hardly taxing for Ramanujan. Therefore Ramanujan would soon finish the job assigned to him, and sit down to work on Mathematics, for which he received encouragement from Sir Francis Spring and his immediate superior S. Narayana Iyer. Most days, Ramanujan will stay up till six in the morning doing Mathematics, sleep for two or three hours and then head to work. This made his life more hectic than to what he used to. Many times, one could see him running to his office with his coat, and everything flying in the breeze with a bright sacred mark *'namam'* on his forehead. It was obvious that he had no time to waste, and therefore was always in hurry.

All through his stay at Madras Port Trust, Ramanujan worked under S. Narayana Iyer, who was the Chief Accountant there. Narayana Iyer, in fact, was not just Ramanujan's immediate superior, boss, or just a colleague but as well his advisor, mentor, and friend. In the evenings, they would retire to the elder man's house on Pycroft's Road in Triplicane. There, they would sit and work often up to midnight, and many times after they both had gone to sleep Ramanujan would wake up and record something that had come to him in the dream, and which he attributed to his Goddess Namagiri of Namakkal.

Ramanujan worked at the Madras Port Trust from March 1, 1912 to May 1, 1913 and on May 1, 1913 he joined the Presidency College, Madras (now Chennai) as a Research Scholar. The details as to how he got the opportunity to be a Research Scholar at the Presidency College of the University of Madras are given later in this book.

□

4

G.H. Hardy—Ramanujan's Mentor, Friend and Guide—Brief Life History

Professor Godfrey Harold Hardy was a renowned British mathematician known for his achievements in number theory and mathematical analysis. He was a brilliant mathematician who also exercised a major influence in other branches of mathematics and on other mathematicians. A whole school had begun to form around him. He had served on the Council of the London Mathematical Society and later occupied numerous other posts in the London Mathematical Society. He is perhaps even better known for his adoption and mentoring of the self-taught Indian mathematical genius, Srinivasa Ramanujan, in whose life and work, he played a pioneering role.

G.H. Hardy

Hardy was born on 7th February, 1877 in Cranleigh, Surrey, England in a rather ordinary family. His father's name was Isaac Hardy and his mother was Sophia Hall. They got married in January 1875. His father Isaac was an assistant master teaching geography and drawing in Cranleigh School. His mother was a senior mistress at Lincoln Diocesan Training College. Earlier, his father had taught in a grammar school in Lincolnshire. Hardy's grandfather had been a laborer and mother's father a baker. Both father and mother were kind and helpful persons. Hardy had a two year younger sister, Gertrude Edith. Both G.H. Hardy and his sister Gertrude never married. In fact Gertrude remained very caring to her brother G.H. Hardy.

4.1 Hardy, a gifted mathematician:

From the very beginning, Hardy was an intellectual genius, but unlike Ramanujan felt no passion for mathematics. When Hardy was two, he could write down numbers into the millions, and, in church, he would entertain himself by finding the prime divisors of the hymn numbers. He studied at Cranleigh School but because of his extraordinary talent in mathematics, he never sat in a regular mathematics class and instead was coached privately by E.T. Clarke, President of the school's mathematics instructions. At the age of nineteen, he passed the high school examination with distinction in mathematics and Latin, and received scholarship at Winchester College. During that time, two universities namely, Cambridge and Oxford, held positions of distinction in England. In 1904, according to a survey, 74% coming from these two universities were holding senior positions enjoying fame in UK. In 1896, Hardy joined Trinity College at Cambridge University.

Hardy was not only a gifted mathematician, but was also a gifted athlete. His first love was mathematics and second was cricket. He even prepared his mathematical papers with analogies to the games. He was a strictly disciplined person in his working style, for example, he devoted only four hours each day from 9:00 a.m. until 1:00 p.m. to mathematical research, leaving the afternoons open for cricket and tennis, and evenings for intellectual discourse. Even as a child, Hardy was an atheist, and as an adult, he refused to enter into houses of worship. To accommodate him, the college wrote a special exemption into its by-laws so that Hardy instead of going to Chapel, could discharge his certain duties by proxy. Hardy believed that God, if it exists, was his personal enemy. Once, on a turbulent boat trip from Scandinavia to England, he dropped a postcard to a mathematician colleague mentioning that he has proved the well-known open conjecture in prime number theory, the Riemann Hypothesis, because he believed that God (whose existence he doubted but to whom he considered his enemy) would not let him die with the people giving him credit of proving Riemann Hypothesis, which he has not. Hardy was a shy man in the sense that he would say nothing other than simply indulging in a small talk or making a polite conversation. In mixed company he may ignore members of other sex unless they happened to be mathematicians. He did not have much of interest in going for ceremonies and formal occasions of all kinds and rarely attended college feasts, but he was very kind to students of all races and colors. Also, he was always very concerned about the interests of the students and would never let them feel down.

In 1730, the 'Tripos' exam had become the index of sharpness in mathematics. The word is pronounced *try-poss* and it originally referred to a three-legged stool, and was regarded as the most difficult mathematical test that the world had ever known. Getting first, second or third position in Tripos was an indication of a very creditable and promising scholar. Philosopher A.N. Whitehead, physicists J.C. Maxwell and J.J. Thomson, Bertrand Russell, Lord Kelvin, J.E. Littlewood, etc. had become famous because of their success in the Tripos exam. At Cambridge, Hardy started preparing for the Tripos examination, in particular from *Course d'Analyse* by Camile Jordan. Hardy was fourth in the Mathematics Tripos examination. Years later, he sought to abolish the Tripos-system, as he felt that it was becoming more an end in itself than a means to an end. While at university, Hardy joined the Cambridge Apostles, an elite, intellectual secret society. In 1901, he was elected to a prize fellowship at Trinity and the prestigious Smith prize along with physicist James Jean.

In 1903 he earned his M.A., which was the highest academic

degree at English universities at that time, from Trinity College, Cambridge, for which he did research under the guidance of A.E.H. Love and E.T. Whittaker. From 1906 to 1919, he held the position of a lecturer at Cambridge University, where teaching only six hours per week left him time for research.

Although, Hardy's own natural affinity for mathematics was perceptible at an early age, however, unlike Ramanujan, there is not much to say on Hardy's research or search questions during student life in school or later. In fact, arising from the controversy between Newton and Leibniz in mathematics, about the founder of calculus, mathematics in England had suffered quite some setback because of Newton's way in national pride. Hardy corrected the position and England fell in line with other European countries. Starting with his first paper in 1899, on definite integrals, he published more than sixty papers on the theory of integration.

4.2 Hardy's Research Areas:

Hardy wrote several books in his life time, but is best known for his book '*A course in Pure Mathematics*', published in 1908. His other three books are '*The Integration of Functions of a Single Variable*' (1905), '*Order of Infinity*' (1910) and jointly with M. Riesz, '*General Theory of Dirichlet Series*' (1915). All these books are also very well-known. His book 'Orders of infinity' is considered to be instrumental in making Ramanujan's decision to write to Hardy about his research.

J. E. Littlewood

From 1911, Hardy started collaborating with J.E. Littlewood, whose full name was John Edensor Littlewood, and did extensive work in mathematical analysis and analytic number theory.

J.E. Littlewood, was born on 9th June, 1885, thus just two years older to Ramanujan, and about eight years younger to Hardy, but he had England's best mathematical education. His father Edward Thornton Littlewood was also a mathematician and was the Ninth Wrangler in the Mathematical Tripos at Cambridge in 1882, just three years before his eldest son, John Edensor was born. In 1892, the family sailed to South Africa where his father Edward Thornton Littlewood accepted the headmastership of a school in Wynberg, Capetown in South Africa.

Although, the climate and scenery in Wynberg, Capetown were superb, but the education that the young Littlewood was receiving in South Africa was not, because of the poor quality of mathematics teachers in the school. He was admitted to the University of Cape Town at a young age but over there also he was not much benefitting from teaching at the university, and therefore in 1900, Littlewood, when aged 15 was sent to England to study at St Paul's School in London. There he had an outstanding teacher of mathematics, Francis Macaulay. While at St Paul's School, in December 1902, Littlewood won a scholarship to Cambridge and in October 1903, he joined Trinity College, Cambridge.

Littlewood spent his first two years preparing for the Tripos examinations which were needed for undergraduates to qualify for a bachelor's degree. In 1905, he obtained the highest marks in Part I of the Tripos examination, and so he became a Senior Wrangler. In 1906, he completed the second part of the Tripos, and started his research under Ernest Barnes. After rapidly solving the problem suggested by his advisor Ernest Barnes, he was suggested to work on proving the Riemann Hypothesis. Although, Littlewood never succeeded in proving Riemann Hypothesis, but he never regretted for that as he felt that by working on this hard problem he could prove several interesting results. In 1908, he was elected as a Fellow of Trinity College, and the same year he won Smith's prize for that year. In 1907, he joined the University of Manchester as the Richardson Lecturer, where after working for about three years at this position, in 1910, he moved to the University of Cambridge, to fill the position vacated by A.N. Whitehead, and later in 1919, he became the Ceyley Lecturer in Cambridge, position vacated by G.H. Hardy. In Cambridge, he worked till his retirement. Littlewood was elected a Fellow of the Royal Society in 1915. He received the Royal Medal of the Society in 1929, and also the Copley Medal of the Royal Society. In 1943, he received the Sylvester Medal of the Society. He received honorary degrees from the University of Liverpool in 1928, the University of St Andrews in 1936 and the University of Cambridge in 1965. He died on September 6, 1977 at the age of 92 years. He is depicted in two films covering the life of Ramanujan—*Ramanujan,* in 2014 portrayed by Michael Lieber and *The Man Who Knew Infinity,* in 2015 portrayed by Toby Jones.

Shortly after joining Cambridge, sometime in 1910 or 1911, he began his famous collaboration with Hardy. Their actual collaboration, in fact, began when the proof in a paper they submitted to London Mathematical Society in June 1911 turned out to be flawed. His collaboration with Hardy lasted for about 35 years during which they worked and wrote a series of papers on the Theory of Series, the Riemann Zeta function, Inequalities, and the Theory of Functions. Hardy and Littlewood were regarded as two most prominent mathematicians in the field of Mathematical Analysis in England.

Hardy's collaboration with Littlewood is considered among the most successful and famous collaborations in mathematical history. Hardy and Littlewood together wrote more than one hundred papers, with their first joint paper appearing in 1912. In a 1947 lecture, the Danish mathematician Harald Bohr reported someone as saying, "Nowadays, there are only three really great English mathematicians: Hardy, Littlewood, and Hardy Littlewood".

Hardy preferred his work to be considered *Pure Mathematics,* perhaps because of his detestation of war and the military uses to which mathematics had been applied. However, his famous work on integer partitions with his collaborator Ramanujan, known as the Hardy-Ramanujan asymptotic formula, has been widely applied in physics to find quantum partition functions of atomic nuclei (first used by Niels Bohr) and to derive thermodynamic functions of non-interacting Bose-Einstein systems. Though Hardy wanted his mathematics to be 'pure' and devoid of any application, much of his work has found applications in other branches of science.

As will be mentioned in the next Chapter, Ramanujan had written to Hardy for help, and Ramanujan's two letters each running in 10 pages, one on 16th January 1913 and the other on 27th February 1913, which he had sent to Hardy, have become a part of history in mathematics. These letters started their interaction and later an invitation was extended to Ramanujan for a visit to England. Ramanujan did come to work with Hardy and during the period of 1914 to 1919, Ramanujan and Hardy spent time together. Concerning Hardy and his interaction with Ramanujan, there is quite some material given separately in the book.

After Ramanujan left Cambridge for India in 1919, Hardy felt lonely which resulted in a gap between research and his life's other activities. He felt not appreciated enough in Cambridge, and so in December 1919, he moved to Oxford as the Savilian Chair of Geometry, and thus became a Fellow of New College at Oxford. His close friend and collaborator J. E. Littlewood succeeded him as the Ceyley Lecturer in Cambridge, with whom the collaboration continued unabated. At Oxford, Hardy felt the freedom in teaching courses of his liking. He spent eleven years and considered those as the happiest period of his life. He in fact created a school in Analysis there, and spent the academic year 1928-1929 at Princeton, in USA.

In 1931, Hardy returned to Cambridge on the Sadleerian Chair succeeding Arthur Cayley and in 1942, he retired from the Sadleerian Chair. He founded the 'Journal of the London Mathematical Society' and also a new series of the 'Oxford Quarterly Journal of Mathematics'.

Hardy received several awards and recognitions. In 1920, he was awarded the Royal Medal of the Royal Society. On 6th March 1929, at the 60th birthday of the famous Norwegian mathematician Abel, Hardy was conferred honors-causa degree by Oslo University in the presence of King of Norway. These honors-causa degrees were conferred on Hardy by several other universities including those from Athens, Harvard, Manchester, Sofia, Birmingham, Edinburgh, etc. On December 27, 1932, he received the prestigious 'Chauvenet award'. He served as Secretary of the London Mathematical Society from 1917 to 1926, and was its President during 1926–1928. Also from the London Mathematical Society he received the highest honor, the De Morgan Medal in 1929. Hardy died on 1st December 1947, the day he was to be presented the Copley Medal of the Royal Society.

Twenty-four persons which include Mary Cartwright, I.J. Good, Edward Linfoot, Cyril Offord, Harry Pitt, Richard Rado, Srinivasa Ramanujan Aiyangar, Robert Rankin, Donald Spencer, Tirukkannapuram Vijayaraghavan, E.C. Titchmarsh, P.L. Srivastava and E.M. Wright completed their research work under Hardy's supervision. Hardy has presently more than 3607 descendants.

Hardy, as mentioned earlier, was a bachelor all his life. He loved to watch cricket and was an avid tennis player. It is said that in his fifties he could even beat the university second string at real tennis, and while in his sixties he could bring off startling shots in cricket.

On one occasion, he gave the following list of his New Year resolutions:

1. Prove the Riemann Hypothesis;
2. Make 211 not out in the fourth innings of the last Test Match at the Oval;
3. Find an argument of the non-existence of God which will convince the general public;
4. Be the first man on top of Mt. Everest;
5. Be proclaimed as the first president of USSR, Great Britain, and Germany;
6. Murder Mussolini.

4.3 Some of Hardy's personal traits:

Being a hard-core atheist, he dismissed the Goddess Namakkal's effect on Ramanujan's research. In an interview by

Paul Erdös, when Hardy was asked what his greatest contribution to mathematics was, Hardy unhesitatingly replied that it was the discovery of Ramanujan. He called their collaboration as "the one romantic incident in my life".

Hardy is well quoted in mathematics. A couple of these mentioned below from *'A Mathematician's Apology'* may well give his way of thinking:

"It is never worth an intelligent man's time to express a majority opinion. By definition, there are already enough people to do that".

"No mathematician should ever allow him to forget that mathematics, more than any other art or science, is a young man's game. Galois died at twenty-one, Abel at twenty seven, Ramanujan at thirty-three, Riemann at forty. There have been men who have done great work later; but I do not know of a single instance of a major mathematical advance initiated by a man past fifty. A mathematician may still be competent enough at sixty, but it is useless to expect him to have original ideas".

"The mathematician's patterns, like the painter's or the poet's must be beautiful; the ideas, like the colors or the words, must fit together in a harmonious way. Beauty is the first test: there is no permanent place in this world for ugly mathematics". It may be very hard to define mathematical beauty, but that is just as true of beauty of any kind---we may not know quite what we mean by a beautiful poem, but that does not prevent us from recognizing one when we read it.

"A mathematician, like a painter or poet, is a maker of patterns. If his patterns are more permanent than theirs, it is because they are made with ideas".

Hardy once told Bertrand Russell "If I could prove by logic that you would die in five minutes, I should be sorry you were going to die, but my sorrow would be very much mitigated by pleasure in the proof".

There are several films made and books written on Hardy and his collaborators J. E. Littlewood, and Ramanujan. Below are mentioned only some of them.

(i) Hardy is a key character, played by Jeremy Irons, in the

2015 movie *The Man Who Knew Infinity,* based on the biography of Ramanujan with the same title by Robert Keningale.

(ii) Hardy is a major character in David Leavitt's fictive biography, *The Indian Clerk* (2007), which depicts his Cambridge years and his relationship with John Edensor Littlewood and Ramanujan.

(iii) Hardy is a secondary character in *Uncle Petros and Goldbach's Conjecture* (1992), a mathematics novel by Apostolos Doxiadis.

□

5

Ramanujan Contacting G.H. Hardy

5.1 Encouragement for Research while on Job:

Ramanujan's simple life, intense dedication and impressive creativity were his great assets in winning unqualified support of people he met. As mentioned earlier, with the help on a well-wisher he got a job of twenty-five rupees per month at the office of the 'Madras Accountant General'. In this capacity, he worked for a couple of weeks only, and on 1st February, 1912, he applied for a job to Chief Accountant of Madras Port Trust. Based on his application, and with the help of Ramachandra Rao, on 1st March, 1912, he got the class three, grade four, post of a clerk in Account Section on thirty rupees per month. Ramachandra Rao has informed later that in this job, the work was rather light, and so after taking care of his official responsibilities, Ramanujan could find enough of time to continue his work on mathematics. Besides, he had the full support and encouragement to continue doing his mathematical researches during office hours also from his immediate superior S. Narayana Iyer and the Madras Port Trust Chairman Sir Francis Spring.

5.2 Correspondence with G.H. Hardy begins:

Ramanujan, on the advice of some real close persons, started writing letters to some eminent mathematicians of Cambridge University. With a letter, he would include some sample results that he had obtained. As one biographer noted, first he wrote to

Henry Baker and E.W. Hobson, both at Cambridge, but they did not respond. Perhaps Ramanujan was, as later developments show, lucky with their 'no', because a 'yes' would have ended in total loss of Ramanujan's career. His Goddess Namagiri was waiting for a God sent mentor that G.H. Hardy turned out to be.

On 16th January 1913, he wrote following letter to Prof. G.H. Hardy. After that he was writing to Hardy at fairly regular intervals until he left for England on 17th March 1914. Having English as a subject right from his early school education had helped in writing these letters. Also, Hardy seemed to remember Ramanujan telling him that his friends had given him some assistance in writing of these letters. However, for Hardy it was Mathematics that mattered, which was surely of Ramanujan.

Dear Sir:

I beg to introduce myself to you as a clerk in the Accounts Department of the Port Trust Office at Madras on a salary of only £20 per annum. I am now about 23 years of age. I have had no University education but I have undergone the ordinary school course. After leaving school I have been employing the spare time at my disposal to work at Mathematics. I have not trodden through the conventional regular course, which is followed in a University course, but I am striking out a new path for myself. I have made a special investigation of divergent series in general and the results I get are termed by the local mathematicians as 'startling'.

Just as in elementary mathematics you give a meaning to a^n when n is negative and fractional to conform to the law which holds when n is a positive integer, similarly the whole of my investigations proceed on giving a meaning to Eulerian Second Integral for all values of n. My friends who have gone through the regular course of University education tell me that $\int^{\infty} x^{n-} e^{-x} dx = \Gamma(n)$ *is true only wher is positive. They say that this integral relation is not true when n is negative. Supposing this is true only* *for positive values of n and also supposing the definition* $n\Gamma(n)=\Gamma(n+1)$ *to be universally true, I have given meanings to these integrals and under the conditions I state the integral is true for all values of n negative and fractional. My whole investigations are based upon this and I have been developing this to a remarkable extent so much so that the local mathematicians are not able to understand me in my higher flights.*

Very recently I came across a tract published by you styled Orders of Infinity in page 36 of which I find a statement. that no definite expression has been as yet found for the number of prime numbers less than any given number. I have found an expression, which very nearly approximates to the real result, the error being negligible. I would request you to go through the enclosed papers. Being poor, if you are convinced that there is anything of value, I would like to have my theorems published. I have not given the actual investigations nor the expressions that I get but I have indicated the lines on which I proceed. Being inexperienced I would very highly value any advice you give me. Requesting to be excused for the trouble I give you.

I remain, Dear Sir,

Yours truly,

S. *Ramanujan*

Added Note: My address is S. Ramanujan, Clerk Accounts Department, Port Trust, Madras, India.

Attached to the letter were 9 pages on which 120 mathematical theorems from algebra, trigonometry, and calculus discovered by him, were written. These were results on evaluating definite integrals, theorems on sum of infinite series, theorems in number theory, theorems on transformation of integrals and series, etc. Taking precaution for not getting abused, he had avoided details and proofs in putting them there. Also, attached to his letter was an offprint of Ramanujan's paper published in 1911, in the *Journal of the Indian Mathematical Society.*

Hardy, at the first look, had problem in understanding the results of Ramanujan as these were quite strange to him, never seen, or imagined! Having had the experience of receiving non-substantial results from some rather fake enthusiasts, claiming to have found some new results, he is reported to have thought that this is work of some similar 'crank Indian mathematician'. The author, it passed his mind could be a 'genius'or a 'fraud'. With a bewildered mind, he kept the papers away and got busy in doing other things.

5.3 Hardy involving Littlewood:

However, as it happened, in his mind, Hardy continued to be intrigued by the results—having never seen anything like or similar to them. He kept thinking over and over but no trace of their being known could occur to him. Before going to sleep that day, he decided that he will show these to his colleague, J.E. Littlewood, and will like to seek his opinion on them. At the time when Ramanujan's letter arrived to Hardy, Littlewood was working at Cambridge University. According to P.C. Snow, Professor Hardy fixed an appointment with Littlewood and both of them met in the Littlewood's room. Littlewood was living in rooms on D-Staircase of Nevile's Court, which was not far from the rooms where Hardy was living. Thus at around 9:00 p.m. on a winter evening in February 1913, they both met and Hardy laid Ramanujan's handwritten sheets on the table. Both started having deep discussions and critical evaluations. Ramanujan had not sent the proofs of the results given therein. So they started working on the proofs of some of these results. Out of those on which attempts were made, some turned out to be new and interesting, while a few others had some errors. Some were in fact, improved and generalized versions of recently obtained results by Hardy.

Both, Hardy and Littlewood, got amazed. By mid-night they arrived at the conclusion that the person having obtained these results is surely a brilliant mathematician. They were also convinced of the genuineness of Ramanujan being the person having obtained these results. The cause of flaws in those results, that were found not correct, they could rightly guess, was the lack of Ramanujan's proper education.

Hardy was so excited to see the work of Ramanujan that he showed those results to a number of people in Cambridge. There was a wave of achievement in the Cambridge University. Hardy sent these results to experts in their fields. They were, in what may be called, mystified at the surprising mathematical fertility of Ramanujan's brain and possibility of his future association with Cambridge.

On this, Bertrand Russell had written to Ottoline Morrell, "In the Hall, I found Hardy and Littlewood in a state of wild excitement, because they believe they have discovered a second Newton, a Hindu clerk in Madras (now Chennai), on 20 pounds a year". Ramanujan wrote to Hardy telling him of some more results he got, which Hardy thinks quite wonderful, especially as the man has had only an ordinary school education. Years later, E.H. Neville wrote:

> *"No one, who was in the mathematical circles in Cambridge at that time, can forget the sensation caused by Ramanujan's letter".*

Eric Harold Neville, was an able, important and young mathematician, who was not as good as Littlewood. At the age of just twenty-five years, he was among the last to take the old-style Tripos—taking it one year early in order to become a Senior Wrangler before Hardy's reforms took place, but he came in second. Two years later, in 1911, he won the Smith's Prize and after one year, in 1912 he became a Fellow of the Trinity College. Around New Year's Day in 1914, he arrived in Madras (now Chennai) to give a series of lectures on Differential Geometry to Mathematics Honors Students at the University of Madras. In addition to delivering lectures at the University of Madras, Hardy entrusted him with the mission of convincing Ramanujan to come to Cambridge.

5.4 Hardy's Response:

Drafting a letter to Ramanujan was not an easy task for Hardy. In fact, he sprang into action to do all that it could take to bring Ramanujan to Cambridge. Besides a letter, he also started taking steps through India Office, and others.

Hardy's letter of 8th February, 1913, full of encouraging words had following contents with brief comments on his results received:

I was exceedingly interested by your letter and the theorems.

You will however understand that before I can judge properly the value of what you have done, it is essential that I should see proofs of some of your assertions. I want particularly to see your proofs of your assertions here. You will understand that, in this theory, everything depends on rigorous exactitude of proof

Assuming your proofs to be rigorous, your results can be classified in three categories, namely,

- *Those that are already known or can be derived from earlier known theorems;*
- *Those that are new even perhaps difficult but not much important;*
- *Those that are new and important.*

Accepting that you lack in proper education, it will be advisable to obtain some results afresh.

Additionally, Prof Littlewood wants to see your formula by which number of prime numbers can be determined. Please send as much proof as possible quickly.

I hope very much that you will send me as quickly as possible a few of your proofs, and follow this more at your leisure by a more detailed account of your work on primes and divergent series.

It seems to me quite likely that you have done a good deal of work worth publication; and if you can produce satisfactory demonstration, I should be very glad to do what I can to secure it.

5.5 Hardy's fast plans to bring Ramanujan to Cambridge:

This letter reached Ramanujan in the third week of February, 1913, but Hardy was so excited to get him to Cambridge that he did not want to have things settled by letters alone. He adopted other channel as well. Through this channel, his endorsement of Ramanujan reached Madras (now Chennai) almost a week before the letter. For this, Hardy had contacted the India Office, and Mr. Mallet had written to Arthur Davis, Secretary of the Advisory Committee for Indian Students in Madras informing him of Hardy's wish to bring Ramanujan to England. Also, Davis met Sir Francis Spring, and through Narayana Iyer had communicated to Ramanujan that Hardy wants Ramanujan to come to Cambridge.

Having learnt Hardy's wish for him to go to Cambridge, Ramanujan's immediate and rather firm response was 'no'. Around the same time Ramanujan was recommended for a scholarship of seventy-five rupees per month to do mathematical research, the details of which will be given later in this chapter.

Hardy's letter had a wider effect on Ramanujan and everyone else in touch with him. In this connection, we find a letter from Secretary of the Indian Students at Cambridge to Secretary to the Advisory Committee for Indian Students, Madras:

> *"I have an enquiry from one of the Mathematical Tutors at Trinity College, Cambridge, about a young Indian called* S. *Ramanujan, who is a Clerk in the Accounts Department of the Port Trust at Madras. It appears that Mr. Ramanujan has sent to the Tutor of Trinity a series of mathematical studies and theorems, which are so remarkable and which show such an extraordinary aptitude for Mathematics, that, if they are his own, as I assume they are, the Tutor in question thinks it possible that he may prove to be a Mathematician of the very highest class. If this be so, it would seem worthwhile enquiring whether some means can be found of getting him a Cambridge education.*
>
> *Would you very kindly make full enquiries and report to me this young man? If the work sent to Cambridge is really his own work, evolved by a man without any University training, we ought to see if anything can be done for him".*

Based on Ramanujan's response on going to England, Arthur Davis on 10th March 1913, formally wrote the following letter to Mr. Bhimen Hanumantha Rao, Chairman of the Board of Studies of Mathematics at the University of Madras:

10th March 1913
"I am directed by my Committee to forward to you the enclosed copy of a letter dated 3rd February, 1913, from the Secretary for Indian Students in London, about a gentleman named S. Ramanujan as it is understood that his case is being considered by the Board of Studies.
Mr. Ramanujan has definitely declined going to England".

5.6 Ramanujan not ready for going to England:

Ramanujan had reasons for not going to England, and we mention below some of them.

The first major response of Ramanujan to say 'no' for going to England, in simple terms could be due to Ramanujan not having given any thoughts about it. Probing further, it is analyzed that the 'no' came up because of some personal and family definite factors. Ramanujan was a married person with a household of parents and two younger brothers. Ramanujan and family were governed by family considerations and religious beliefs. Some Hindu books of law, called *smirities,* advise against crossing the seas.

It may be mentioned that the Hindu smrities's vague advise against traveling overseas is in fact meant 'to avoid pollution'. The word, pollution may have been used in rather very uncertain terms physical, mental and ethical. Crossing the seas was considered in the same category as publicly discarding the sacred thread or eating beef.

Over the long history of Indian invasions and Indians taken as 'slaves' being in vogue in the outer world, and also the polluting norms, practices and emotional causes, this may have evolved. For recent recordable social history in India, around that time, Mahatma Gandhi, and the first President of independent India Dr. Rajendra Prasad, and also mathematician Professor Ganesh Prasad faced this injunction. In Hinduism, there is no practice like Christian 'confession'. A little hard and more effective is one that of atonement *(paschatap)* and a harder one practiced in the past, no longer in practice is that of 'excommunication'. As an example, in 1888, on the eve when Mahatma Gandhi was departing for London to study law, the elders of his caste forbade the journey on the grounds that the rules prohibited traveling abroad. They could not, among other things, permit him to eat and drink with Europeans. Gandhi refused to obey and was excommunicated. As a result, Gandhi found that on his return, three years later, from England his closest relatives were forbidden to receive him in their homes, even for a drink of water. He never sought readmission to his caste. This experience in fact led him to a broader view of caste system than most Hindus held. As a result, he was never troubled by castes, and this made his task easier when he insisted on having a family of untouchables live in his Sabarmati Ashram in India.

About caste system in India, Gandhi had the view (see, Shirer [17, p. 112] in Section 14.2) "Some argue that the retention of the caste system spells ruin for India and it is the caste which has reduced India to slavery. In my opinion, it is not caste that India has made us what we are. It was our greed and disregard of essential virtues, which enslaved us. I believe that the caste has saved Hindustan from disintegration". Also, he mentions "I do believe in Varna [caste], which is based on hereditary occupations: imparting knowledge, defending the defenseless, carrying agriculture and commerce, and performing service through labor. These occupations are common to all mankind. I consider the four caste divisions alone fundamental, natural and essential".

Ramanujan's parents, in particular his mother is reported to have been strictly against his going across the seas. Apart from these apprehensions, Ramanujan having no university degree meaning there by to be a student again and to appear in some exams thereafter. Apparently these can be put as:

- He was a strict vegetarian and had been following the practice of not eating food cooked by an unknown person.
- He was not confident of his knowledge in English, having failed in it at earlier exams.
- Fear of entering again in University education for a degree, learning things to pass some exams, having flunked exams before.

Apart from family and the above cultural and personal reasons, a strong contributing factor was also, the way a common Indian, that Ramanujan, was being handled by British public offices, in this case, the 'India Office'. Ramanujan was not duly informed of the financial support and of what he will be required to do in Britain. In view of these, he preferred to stay in Madras (now Chennai) on some kind of scholarship and tried for that. This can be seen in his following letter dated 27th February, 1913 of Ramanujan to G.H. Hardy:

27th February, 1913

I am very much gratified on perusing your letter of 8th February 1913. I have found a friend in you who views my labors sympathetically.

What I want at this stage is for eminent professor like you to recognize that there is some worth in me, which encourages me now to proceed onward. For my results are verified to be true even though I may take my stand upon slender basis.

If I had given you my methods of proof I am sure you will follow the London Professor. But as a fact, I did not give him any proof but made some assertions as the following under my new theory. I told him that the sum of the infinite no. of terms of the series:1+2+3+4+... =-1/12 under my theory. If I tell you this, you will at once point out to me the lunatic asylum as my goal. I dilate on this simply to convince you that you will not be able to follow my methods of proof if I indicate the lines on which I proceed in a single letter. You may ask how you can accept results based upon wrong premises. What I tell you is this: Verify the results I give and if they agree with your results, got by treading on the groove in which the present day mathematicians move, you should at least grant that there is some truths in my fundamental basis.

I am already a half-starving man. To preserve my brains I want food and this is now my first consideration. Any sympathetic letter from you will be helpful to me here to get a scholarship either from the University or from Government.

I have also given meaning to the fractional and negative no. of terms in a series as well as in a product, and I have got theorems to calculate such values exactly and approximately. Many wonderful results have been got from such theorems...

You may judge me hard that I am silent on the methods of proof I do not mean that the methods should be buried with me.

5.7 Research Scholarship at Madras University:

As mentioned above, Hardy, in addition to the encouraging letter to Ramanujan, had communicated through other channels his interest in helping Ramanujan. His endorsements had reached 'India Office', and from there to Sir Francis Spring and Narayana Iyer. Hardy's letter had served the purpose of strong credential to Ramanujan.

Gilbert Walker, was a first-class mathematician trained at Cambridge. He was a Fellow of the Royal Society, and was classed as a Senior Wrangler in Part I of the Mathematical Tripos in 1889. He was a Fellow of the Trinity College, Cambridge during 1891-1904 and served as Director-General of Indian Observatories from 1904 to 1924, as well as the Head of the Indian Meteorological Department in Shimla. The observatory was located in the district of Madras (now Chennai), on the south bank of the river Cooum, about two-and-half-miles from the Bay of Bengal. He was an applied mathematician and did write a paper, "The Cold Weather Storms of Northern India", and is considered as the father of monsoon studies in India, which has affected the lives of the people in India. When Walker was passing through Madras (now Chennai) on 25th February, 1913, Sir Francis showed him the work of Ramanujan. He immediately recognized the intrinsic quality of the work of Ramanujan, and next day, on 26th February Walker wrote to the Registrar of Madras University, describing Ramanujan's work comparable in originality with that of a mathematics fellow in the Cambridge College, although lacking in precision and completeness. In his letter that is produced below, he suggested granting a research fellowship to Ramanujan, so that Ramanujan for a few years at least could spend the whole of his time on Mathematics without any anxiety as to his livelihood.

Gilbert T. Walker to Francis Dewsbury, Registrar of the University of Madras.

26 February 1913
Madras

To
The Registrar University of Madras
Sir:
I have the honor to draw your attention to the case of S. Ramanujan, a clerk in the Accounts Department of the Madras Port Trust. I have not seen him, but was yesterday shown some of his work in the presence of Sir Francis Spring. He is, I am told, 22 years of age and the character of the work that I saw impressed me as comparable in originality with that of a mathematics fellow in the Cambridge College; it appears to lack, however, as might be expected in the circumstances and precision necessary before the universal validity of the results could be accepted. I have not specialized in the branches of pure mathematics at which he has worked, and could not therefore form a reliable estimate of his abilities, which might be of an order to bring him a European reputation. But it was perfectly clear to me that the university would be justified in enabling S. Ramanujan for a few years at least to spend the whole of his time on Mathematics without any anxiety as to his livelihood, and I would suggest that they should communicate with Mr. G. H Hardy, Fellow of Trinity College, Cambridge with whom he is already in correspondence and assure Mr. Hardy of their interest in him.
I have the honor to be, Sir

Your most obedient servant
Gilbert T. Walker,
Director General of Observatories

As a follow up of Mr. Walker's letter, Hanumantha Rao held a meeting on 19th March of the Board of Studies in Mathematics inviting Narayana Iyer to discuss the award of scholarship to Ramanujan. In this meeting, the board recommended to Syndicate, the university's governing body for awarding research scholarship of seventy-five rupees per month for two years.

Six weeks after Hardy's letter, the Syndicate met on April 7, 1913 and Ramanujan's case came up. However, it faced difficulty from some member's opposing, because research scholarships were meant to be awarded to those candidates who have a master's degree, while Ramanujan did not have even a bachelor's degree. It is reported that Oxford educated Professor of Mathematics Richard Littlehailes at Presidency College strongly supported Ramanujan's case for the award of a scholarship. The Chancellor, P.R. Sundaram, Chief Justice of Madras High Court, invoked the preamble of the University for promoting research. The inadequacies of Ramanujan's education were stretched and relaxed in view of his credentials as a mathematical researcher. This argument carried the day. The Registrar recorded, "The regulations of the University do not at present provide for such a special scholarship. But the Syndicate assumes that Section XV of the Act of lncorporation and Section 3 of the Indian Universities Act, 1904, allow of the grant of such a scholarship, subject to the express consent of the Governor of Fort St. George in the Council", which the university received without any delay.

As a result of all these, the Board of Studies of the University of Madras granted to Ramanujan a special research scholarship of seventy-five rupees per month (Ramanujan's pay was only thirty rupees per month when he was working at the Madras Port Trust, and the Professor's pay in the university those days used to be around two hundred twenty-five rupees per month) for two years subject to obtaining approval of the Government of the Madras Presidency.

On April 12, 1913, Ramanujan got the information of this award, and on May 1, 1913, he was relieved from his clerical post from the office of Madras Port Trust, and joined as Research Scholar at the Presidency College, Madras (now Chennai). The

Madras Port Trust granted him leave without pay for two years so that he could avail this scholarship during that period.

In fact, Ramanujan was the first research scholar of the University of Madras, and this became the beginning of his research career as a professional mathematician, on which he remained all his life. The only requirement for Ramanujan to hold this scholarship was that he will submit quarterly reports of his work, which he submitted on 5th August 1913, 7th November 1913 and 9th March 1914 respectively, before leaving for England. Unfortunately, the University of Madras has lost the original quarterly reports but a handwritten copy of these reports was made by T.A. Satagopan in 1925. Later, G.N. Watson made handwritten copies of these reports and it is believed that copies of both these reports are in the Cambridge University Library.

Ramanujan, now having scholarship moved with his wife, mother and maternal grandmother to his residence, from house located in George Town to one on Hanumantharayan Koil Street, situated about one-and-a-half mile from Presidency College. The house was also close to 'Parthasarthy temple'.

Ramanujan now had a separate room upstairs in the house for his work. Day and night he was busy in his research work. During the early morning hours, and later at night, his earlier superior, now a sincere friend Narayana Iyer would come to work on mathematics with him. Frequently, they would go to Connemara Library that had a section housing university book for carrying their studies. Janaki in her interviews has remarked, "he (Ramanujan) would ask his mother or grandmother to wake him up after midnight so that he could go on with his work in the silent and cooler hours of the after-night".

Ramanujan was about 26 years of age then. His wife Janaki took good care of him but was not able to share much with him intellectually. Once by taking water in a jug and using a tube, Ramanujan demonstrated a siphon experiment, showing how gravity drew the water to lower levels. Ramanujan was fond of food cooked by his mother.

He submitted his progress report regularly every three months. The first report after the award was sent on 5th August,

1913. A theorem that he included in this report later became famous as *'Ramanujan's Master Theorem'.* Using this theorem, a number of definite integrals could be easily evaluated. Based on this *'Frullani Integral Theorem'* was a generalization of one in Hardy's paper published in 1902.

5.8 Exchange of letters between Hardy and Ramanujan continued:

While steps were being taken for offering research scholarship to Ramanujan, there continued exchange of letters between Ramanujan and Hardy. Professor Hardy kept on requesting Ramanujan for proofs of his results, and Ramanujan, offering excuses, continued to hold back the proofs. Ramanujan not complying with proofs, became irritating and, on this Littlewood once wrote to Hardy, "I rather suspect he's afraid that you will steal his results". This was plainly conveyed by Hardy to Ramanujanin in his letter of 26th March, 1913, in following terms:

> *"Since I wrote to you last I have heard from Mr. Littlewood to whom I sent your last letter, and I have considered further some of your results.......*
>
> *Mr. Littlewood suggested to me also that your unwillingness to give proofs was probably due to apprehensions as to the use I might make of your results. Let me put the matter plainly to you. You have in your possession now 3 long letters of mine, in which I speak quite plainly about what you have proved or claim to be able to prove. I have shown your letters to Mr. Littlewood, Dr. Barnes, Mr. Berry, and other mathematicians. Surely it is obvious that if I were to attempt to make any illegitimate use of your results, nothing will be easier for you than to expose me. You will, I am sure, excuse my stating the case with such bluntness. I should not do so if I were not genuinely anxious to see what can be done to give you a better chance of making the best use of your obvious mathematical gifts.*

This letter was followed by Ramunjan's following letter of 17th April, 1913:

17th April, 1913

Dear Sir,

I am in receipt of your letter of the 26th March. I am a little pained to see what you have written at the suggestion of Mr. Littlewood. I am not in the least apprehensive of my method being utilized by others. On the contrary my method has been in my possession for the last eight years and I have not found anyone to appreciate the method. As I wrote in my last letter I have found a sympathetic friend in you and I am willing to place unreservedly in your possession what little I have. It was on account of the novelty of the method I have used that I am a little diffident even now to communicate my own way of arriving at the expressions I have already given. But still in this letter I have attempted to give a demonstration which would be acceptable to you all.

You speak of having written to me three long letters. But I have received only two......... I am anxious to know what your other communication contained I am glad to inform you that the local University has been pleased to grant me a scholarship of pounds 60 per annum for two years and this was at the instance of Dr. Walker FRS Head of the Meteorological Department in India to whom my thanks are due. The scholarship will help me a great deal for two years.

My knowledge of English being poor I find it difficult my thoughts and put them in a form presentable to you. I have tried this time to give you a proof in connection with the expression I have for the distribution of primes.......

I am delighted to hear that not only yourself but also other mathematicians at the very fountain head of mathematical knowledge are interesting themselves in my humble work. I request you to convey my thanks not only to your good self but also Mr. Littlewood, Dr. Barnes, Mr. Berry and others who take an interest in me.

I am

Yours very sincerely
S. Ramanujan

Ramanujan's this and earlier communications with some proofs were with Hardy, and he jointly with Mr. Littlewood was verifying their validity. In his letter of 24th December, 1913 to Ramanujan, Hardy made detailed comment showing incompleteness and error in the Ramanujan's proofs and results, softly concluding the long letter as follows:

"[as regards theory of primes] The truth is that the theory of primes is full of pitfalls, to surmount which requires the fullest trainings in modern rigorous methods. This you are naturally without. I hope you will not be discouraged by my criticism. I think your argument a very remarkable and ingenious one. To have proved what you claimed to have proved would have been about the most remarkable mathematical feat in the whole history of mathematics.

As regards your work on continued fractions and elliptic functions—here the difficulties to be surmounted are of an entirely different kind, and I have no reason at all to suppose that your results are not perfectly correct. I hope you will adopt the suggestions I made at the beginning.

Try to make the acquaintance of Mr. E. H. Neville, who is now in Madras lecturing. He comes from my college and you might find his advice as to reading and study invaluable.

Well, you will see from the length of this letter that answering yours is not an entirely trifling business and that I have some excuse if I have delayed. Believe me.

Yours very sincerely
G.H. Hardy

5.9 Developments -for Ramanujan going to England:

Hardy was very much disappointed at Ramanujan's refusal to go to Cambridge, and for this reason he had been at regular intervals writing persuasive letters pointing to Ramanujan the advantages of a short visit to Cambridge. But, early in 1914, when the University of Madras invited Mr. E.H. Neville, he met Ramanujan and won his confidence so that Ramanujan could give him his Notebooks.

E.H. Neville

He saw his priceless Notebooks and after taking a look at the Notebooks he was convinced of Ramanujan's uncommon ability and wanted to take charge of taking him to England. For this he took over the initiative to overcome all the difficulties, including arranging a scholarship to bear all the expenses associated with Ramanujan's visit. After meetings with Neville, Ramanujan's initial decision for not going to England as proposed by Hardy, underwent change. In the following letter of Ramanujan to Hardy, reasons mentioned above were later advanced by Ramanujan. In this letter, he clearly conveys his change of mind—decision to go to England. It is interesting to analyze the reasons for this change, given after this letter.

22 January, 1914

"Now I learn from your letter and Mr. Neville that you are anxious to get me to Cambridge....... If you had written to me previously, I would have expressed my thoughts plainly to you."

The Chairman of the Port Trust told my superior officer to go with me and answer his questions. He asked me whether. I was prepared to go to England. While I was hesitating to reply him as the questions appeared vague to me. I naturally was thinking whether I had to appear for any examination with my very poor educational qualification as I used to see students from here going to England only for appearing for some examination, my superior officer, a very orthodox Brahman having scruples to go to foreign land replied at once that I could not go to England and the matter was dropped.

...... Another thing I have to say to you is that all letters written to you, except this one did not contain my language. Those were written by my superior officer mentioned before, though the mathematical results and handwriting were my own. I am writing these things plain to you so that you may judge properly my knowledge of English and power of expression of thoughts as they are.

I went to Mr. Neville of your college who very kindly spoke to me and cleared my doubts that I need not care for my expenses, that my English will do, that I am not asked to go to England to appear for any examination and that I can remain a vegetarian there. He also pointed out to me the benefits I derive in coming in contact with modern mathematicians and modern ways of thinking. Then when I expressed my willingness to go there he said that the best time for me to go there is summer and it will be difficult for me to go there in winter.

So I request that you and Mr. Littlewood will be good enough to take the trouble of getting me there within a very few months".

The reasons for change in his case, on deeper analysis can be put in the following two categories:

- The psychological ones which needed some divine prompting, that was at the back of all functions and thoughts of Ramanujan;
- Some fears about life in England and arrangement of finances to travel and live there.

Ramanujan and his all-important mother needed to undergo change in favor of a travel to England. This happened through two 'dreams'or 'divine visions'.

According to Neville, Ramanujan's mother saw a dream in

which Ramanujan is surrounded with Europeans. In the dream, according to Neville, Goddess Namagiri instructed the mother not to be an obscuration in the path of her son's life purpose by going abroad.

According to another account, it was Goddess Namagiri in her temple at Namakkal to have instructed Ramanujan for no hesitation for overseas travel. Towards end of December 1913, Ramanujan, his mother, Mr. Narayana Iyer and son of Narayana Iyer took train to go to Namakkal. However, they got down at Salem and stayed at the house of Mr. Ramaswamy Iyer, who had founded the 'Indian Mathematical Society' and was a Deputy Collector over there. From there Ramanujan went to his hometown Kumbakonam and after that, with Narayana Iyer, set out to Namakkal, which had the shrine of Goddess Namagiri. On their way, they perhaps rode on bullock-cart. First they reached at the gate of the temple, which on the right had a statue of 'God Narasimha (Narasimha, 'one of the ten, in fact fourth, reincarnations of Vishnu), and on the left had a shrine of Goddess Namagiri.

For three days, they both stayed in the temple and slept on the floor of the temple. Nothing unusual happened on the first two nights. However on the third night, Ramanujan woke-up from a dream, woke Mr. Narayana Iyer, and mentioned to him that in the midst of lightening, he received a 'divine order' not to accept any injunction against foreign travel. This made Ramanujan free from incurring any '*papa*' (guilt) of crossing over the seas.

As regards the problems of the second category, which were also substantial not addressed to earlier, were amicably resolved by Neville, who met Ramanujan and they talked as follows:

Ramanujan—How about the financial arrangement?

Neville—Do not worry for that. All due arrangements will be made!

Ramanujan—My English is not good!

Neville—This is not so. That is good enough.

Ramanujan—I am a vegetarian!

Neville—That will continue to be respected.

Ramanujan—And what about examinations?

Neville—You will not be required to undertake any examination.

These events settled almost all matters for Ramanujan's going to England. But there were others. Some friends of Ramanujan were not happy for a person who was the pride of Madras (now Chennai) to go away to England. On this Neville said that Ramanujan is going in his own interest, and this will increase the pride of both India and England.

Ramanujan's father-in-law was in favor of his continuing to do mathematics in India. His mother was still worried about his health in the cold climate, and also about proper arrangement for his food. She was afraid of the loss of social status, for having traveled abroad. There was also apprehension in her mind about Ramanujan coming in touch with English women, having seen some English women shaking hands with him, which she did not like.

5.10 Problem of finances for going:

After having all issues cleared with Ramanujan, Neville applied himself to fix financial matters. He wrote to Hardy of the developments and therein said, "it was now time to address the financial obstacles to Ramanujan's visit to England". In this connection he further added, that he would try to find money from India Office, Madras (now Chennai), but in the event of being unsuccessful, the money must somehow be found in England. When the case was referred to India Centre, its Secretary Mr. C. Mallet, on February 11, 1914 wrote:

> *Dear Mr. Hardy,*
> *I quite understand your letter, and sympathize with it, but money is the vital point. I know of no means from which sufficient money is forthcoming to bring Mr. Ramanujan home to Cambridge, even for two years.... I am quite clear that no money for this purpose can be got from the India Office, and I should have thought it doubtful—though on this point you know it better than I—whether Trinity College or Cambridge University was likely to find money for the purpose....... We have known so many cases of Indian students, brought over here in the vague hope that*

somehow or other money would be found to keep them in England with the inevitable result of disappointment and misery for them.

I would tell him [Mr. Neville} that the India Office can find no money for such a purpose, and I think I would remind him, if you agree, that Cambridge is very unlikely to do so.

Yours sincerely
C. Mallet
Secretary for Indian Students

This letter must have frightened Mr. Hardy and in that state he wrote the following letter around 12th February, 1914, to Mr. Neville:

Dear Neville,

I am writing in a hurry to catch the mail and warn you to be a little careful. I've been in correspondence with the India Office again—I enclose the last letter. In order that Ramanujan should come—and of that I'm as anxious as ever—there must be absolute certainty of about £250 a year. When I wrote to them before they left me under the impression that could certainly be found (not from the India Office here—there is not and never was any question of that). The sources contemplate were, I presume, Madras University or the Central Government of India. According to their then version, Ramanujan's reluctance was the only obstacle. Now this man Mallet seems disposed to sing a different tune. So be very cautious. I think JE.L. and I between us could contribute £50 for 2 years (don't tell Ramanujan so)—but that's only a very little way.

...... Please keep me well informed as to the progress of the attempts to raise money in India: but don't pledge yourself to anything uncertain,

Ever yours
G.H. Hardy

Neville, in the above letter from Hardy, inferred Hardy's cold feet and timidity. He attributed it to the fact that "Hardy has neither talked to Ramanujan nor has seen his Notebooks, while I have seen". Before receiving this letter, Neville's efforts for financial support had already advanced. Oxford educated Mr. Richard Littlehailes, was mathematics faculty at Presidency College and based on the provision had opposed the award of scholarship to Ramanujanam. He had introduced Neville to some very senior and influential persons in the University and the Government. They had spoken to the University Registrar Mr. Francis Dewsbury, and on 28th January 1914, Neville wrote a very strong letter to Mr. Francis Dewsbury mentioning the importance of securing a training to Ramanujan in the refinements of modem methods and a contact with men who know what range of ideas have been explored and what have not. He further professed that Ramanujan would respond to such a stimulus and that his name will become one of the greatest in the history of mathematics, and the University and City of Madras (now Chennai) will be proud to have assisted in his passage from obscurity to fame.

The very next day, on 29th January 1914, Professor Littlehailes wrote to the Registrar Mr. Francis Dewsbury asking Dewsbury "to arrange for a 250-pound scholarship per year with additional 100 pound grant for Western clothes and for passage to England. He wrote, "Ramanujan is a man of most remarkable mathematical ability, amounting I might say to genius, whose light is metaphorically hidden under bushel in Madras (now Chennai)".

The proposal regarding the scholarship to be granted for gomg to Cambridge was approved within a week by the University of Madras. The University Syndicate decided to set aside Rupees Ten Thousand, to offer Ramanujan, as requested, a scholarship of 250 pounds a year, along with 100 pounds for the passage by ship and western clothes.

The matter reached before Governor of Madras, Lord Pentland with highlighted credentials of Ramanujan, and at the instance of Professors Neville and Littlehails, Sir Francis Spring wrote to Mr. C.B. Cotterell, the personal secretary to the Governor of Madras, to persuade His Excellency to speedily approve the

University's sanction. The Governor's approval was also obtained and thus Ramanujan had a scholarship of 250 pounds, out of which 50 pounds per year were allotted to support his family in India, and exhibition of 60 pounds from Trinity. For Ramanujan having very simple tastes, this grant was sufficient and in fact from this scholarship was able to save a good amount of money, which was used later.

□

6

Ramanujan's Departure to Cambridge and Journey on Ship

After the scholarship for going to England was approved for Ramanujan, it became clear that he was going to England, and that he was going by himself, and that his wife, Janaki was not accompanying him. In fact, one day Ramanujan was at the temple with his mother, mother-in-law, and wife Janaki. Then Janaki asked Ramanujan if she could accompany him on his trip to England, on which Ramanujan said "no". Further, perhaps to make his reply humorous and interesting he told Janaki that she being so young and pretty he is afraid that some Englishman would get attracted to her and may take her away.

6.1 Getting familiar to British ways:

About a week before his departure, Ramanujan sent his wife and mother to Kumbakonam for which he bid them farewell at Madras's (now Chennai's) Egmore railway station, so that they do not have to see his transformation into a European style gentleman. This included changing the traditional hair-style of the Brahmin, viz. his long 'tuft', the long bunched-up knot of hair at the back of his head to go, and his hair trimmed in European style. Further, he was given training in wearing western clothes, and was provided with help in making purchases of shirts, collars and ties, stockings and shoes, etc. Also, for few days, Ramanujan had to stay at the house of a friend of Ramachandra Rao, who had been living European-style, so that he may be trained in using knife and fork. With all this, Ramanujan was in fact not very happy since he preferred eating by hands, and did not relish food being served by servants, and eating with spoon, knife and fork.

Srinivasa Ramanujan

On February 26, 1914, Binny & Co. sent to Ramanujan his second-class ticket. Ramanujan was to depart by British India Lines Ship S.S. Nevasa, which was almost brand-new, and was designed especially to run for India route. Her hull was in black paint, except for red accents and a thin ribbon of white running fore and aft. She was a smart-looking vessel and graceful in every way. Barely a year had passed since she had been delivered to Binny & Co. by a Glasgow shipyard. She was about 9000 tons, and was the largest ship in the British India Lines fleet.

On March 11, 1914, Sir Francis Spring wrote to the steamer agents to make sure that Ramanujan was served vegetarian food on the way. Ramanujan was in fact worried about how he would stay vegetarian in England but was assured by E.H. Neville that he will be provided vegetarian food over there and that there would be no problem in that. Ramanujan did not appear to be happy with his westerns style haircut and the clothes he was to wear, and in particular with the knot on his tie, which he did not find comfortable.

On 15th March 1914, the British India Lines Ship S.S. Nevasa arrived at the Madras Port, and was to depart back for England on March 17, 1914. Ramanujan was to go by this ship. On the morning of 17th March, the day ship was to depart, an official send-off was held in the honor of Ramanujan. This was organized by Srinivasa Iyenger, the Advocate General, and was attended by several dignitaries which included Professor Middlemast, Sir Francis Spring, some of the prominent judges, and Kasturirangar Iyengar, publisher of the daily newspaper "Hindu". Also included in this send-off were Ramanujan's mentor and former boss at Madras Port Trust, S. Narayana Iyer, who put a proposal to Ramanujan to exchange Ramanujan's slate with his slate, to which Ramanujan gladly agreed. S. Narayana Iyer's son later told that his father did this because he thought this would provide him some inspiration to do Mathematics during Ramanujan's absence.

Ramanujan was also introduced to Mr. J.H. Stone, the Director of Public Instruction of the Government of Madras, who wished him all the success. Mr. Stone told Ramanujan that he has written to some of his friends about him, and that they would take care of him in England. Besides, Ramanujan met several passengers, which included a man associated with the Salvation Army, and Dr. Muthu, a specialist in Tuberculosis. Ramanujan was also greeted by the Captain of the ship who jokingly mentioned that they will get along fine as long as Ramanujan did not bother him with his Mathematics. Although, everyone was cheerful and proud with the success of Ramanujan, and his going to England to work with Hardy at Cambridge, but Ramanujan did not appear to be so happy. He was in fact, sad and in tears.

6.2 Sailing to Britain:

As scheduled, Ramanujan sailed by the ship Nevasa in the morning of 17th March 1914, leaving his wife, friends and family in India. Although, the ship Nevasa was the largest ship of the British India Lines, with nine thousand tons of weight, but still Ramanujan was not feeling very comfortable. In fact, this being his first ocean voyage, he felt seasick and was unable to eat. However, he got some relief when the ship took her first stop in Colombo, capital of Sri Lanka, an island just few miles off from India's southeast coast.

On March 19, 1914, the ship steamed out of Colombo port for a weeks'passage across the Arabian Sea to the port of Aden, a distance of more than two thousand miles, and in this voyage, Ramanujan felt much better. He had his vegetarian food, met several of other passengers, and enjoyed the ship's roominess. Accordingly, in one week on March 26, 1914, he reached Aden. From Aden began about fourteen-hundred-mile passage to Suez in Red Sea where the ship reached on March 29, 1914. This was a difficult passage because during this journey, the ship got almost baked in a desert heat with temperature never going below hundred degrees, and this made the starboard cabins, in particular, very hot. After staying for a day at Suez, the ship Nevasa left on 30th March for Port Said on other side of the Suez Canal, where it reached on March 31.

From Suez, Ramanujan posted several letters back to India, among them, one to Viswanatha Sastri, and one to R. Krishna Rao, nephew of Ramachandra Rao who had greatly helped Ramanujan in arranging a meeting with his uncle Ramachandra Rao. It was Ramachandra Rao who provided Ramanujan financial help of Rupees twenty-five per month to devote fulltime in mathematical research without worrying of livelihood.

The letter Ramanujan wrote to R. Krishna Rao is produced below (see the book by Berndt and Rankin [4, pp. 106-107] in Section 14.2 of this book).

30 March 1914
Suez

Dear Mr. Krishna Rao,
Reached Suez this evening. The steamer arrived on 15th at Madras and I was very busy the next day (sending my people to Kumbakonam after packing up things, going to Wrenn Bennett to buy things, to the College, town, etc.) and so I couldn't go to you; but I told your brother to inform you of my starting on 1st morning and thought I could see you at the Harbour.
For the first three days I was very uncomfortable and took very little food and after that I have been alright. The sea is very smooth and there is no fear of sea sickness. I do not know whether I have to go to Cambridge directly or stay at London and then go. I shall write to you after I reach England and everything is definitely settled. My best compliments to your brother and respects and warmest thanks to your uncle.
I am
Yours very sincerely,
S. Ramanujan

PS: Wrenn Bannett was a British-owned, department store located on General Patters Road near Triplicane.

The next day, the Nevasa left Port Said, steaming into Mediterranean reaching Genoa on 6th April, and next day on 7th April 1914, Ramanujan wrote another letter to his home.

6.3 Arriving in England:

After leaving Genoa, S.S. Nevasa docked first at Plymouth, and then by steaming through English Channel, on Tuesday, April 14, 1914, arrived at the mouth of Thames. Those days, London had a population of about five million people, almost ten times more than that of Madras (now Chennai), which was the capital of south India. On the other hand, London was in a way capital of the world, and it was from here that the empire was directed. It was a strange new world for anyone off the boat from India, and so was for Ramanujan.

Back home, the Englishmen that Ramanujan had known were all educated and belonged to upper class, but in London he saw all sorts of Englishmen, like lamplighters who patrolled the streets at dusk with long poles, knife grinders manning little two-wheeled carts, men selling muffins, and women both in finery and in rags. He also saw double-decker buses with signs advertising Nestle's chocolate, and other commodities.

According to Neville's younger brother Raymond, when Nevasa arrived at the dock, it was a bright, lovely day, little warmer than usual, and just two days after Easter. Londoners were enjoying by taking full advantage of this sunny and warmer day. At the docks when Ramanujan disembarked from Nevasa, Neville and his older brother who had a Jowett car were waiting to receive him. He was then driven in that Jowett car, that belonged to the Neville's older brother, to the Office of Educational Advisor to Indian Students, which was located at 21 Cromwell Road, in the South Kensington, district of London. This place served as a reception center for Indian students just arriving in England.

Cromwell Road, to which Neville had taken Ramanujan, had office of the National Indian Association. Also, over there was a building, where several rooms were available to students passing through, and for few days, Neville put Ramanujan in one of those rooms. The stay at Cromwell Road was supposed to ease the transition for the students coming fresh from India, but in case of Ramanujan it really didn't.

Fortunately, Ramanujan had Neville by his side to ease the transition. Over there he also met A.S. Ramalingham, a twenty-three years old engineer from Madras (now Chennai), who had been in England for four years. Ramalingham also tried to help Ramanujan feel home. After staying for few days at Cromwell Road, on 18th April, Ramanujan went with Neville to Cambridge. Neville was living on 113 Chestertown Road, a little suburb of Cambridge just across the River Cam from the town itself. Ramanujan soon settled in Neville's house.

Neville's house was a modest two story building first built

around 1850, and had been enlarged, by adding a third story which provided three more rooms. Neville and his new wife Alice had moved in this house just about a year ago, sometime in 1913. The house was quite spacious and at the back of the house was a large garden, which had once been probably a pear orchard. Ramanujan got settled in this house, where he enjoyed a measure of privacy which he had never enjoyed before. Also, while sitting in the second-floor sitting room, Ramanujan could look out and had a view over the River Cam, and Victoria Bridge. Staying at Neville's house was Ramanujan's first introduction to an English home and here he stayed for about two months.

Now having settled in Neville's house, Ramanujan had of course some business to attend to, like paying of fees, and paperwork to do, which was taken care of by Hardy and Neville. Hardy paid twenty pounds to the college for his entrance and other fees, and made arrangements so that he gets a scholarship of forty pounds per year. In the meantime, Ramanujan was now set to work with Hardy and Littlewood. He already started working very hard, and was seeing Littlewood about once a week but to Hardy more often. He was now very happy and productive because of his now being in the right environment, something he had been looking for, and thus in a way had everything that he had desired.

Whewell's Court, Trinity College, Cambridge

Although, Ramanujan was very happy and comfortable living in Neville's house, but it was about twenty-minute walk to the New Court at the Southwestern edge of the college, where Hardy lived. Therefore in early June, after living for about six weeks with Neville at Chestertown Road, Ramanujan moved to Whewell's Court, from where it was only a five-minute walk to the place where Hardy lived. Ramanujan was really sad to leave Neville's house, because Neville was the first Englishman to win Ramanujan's confidence, and from the moment he disembarked from the ship, Neville had done everything to make him comfortable in the English life. But for Ramanujan, there was no choice but to make this move for the sake of his work, as his staying with Neville was inconvenient for both, Ramanujan, and Professors Hardy and Littlewood.

Hardy and Littlewood began their collaboration with Ramanujan by looking at this notebooks that he had brought from India. Hardy already had more than 120 theorems which Ramanujan had sent with his two letters that he wrote from India, but in addition to these there were many more results and theorems in the notebooks that Ramanujan brought with him to England.

It may be noted that Ramanujan brought with him three notebooks of loose-leaf papers that mostly contained just the results, with no derivation. The first notebook had 351 pages having 16 somewhat organized chapters along with some more material, which was not so organized. The second notebook had 256 pages containing 21 chapters, in addition to another about 100 unorganized pages, while the third notebook had only 33 pages, which were again not organized. Hardy found some of the theorems in the notebooks to be wrong, some of the theorems already been discovered, while the rest were new breakthrough. This work of Ramanujan left a great impression on Hardy and Littlewood, and once, Littlewood even commented that "I can believe that he is at least Jacobi" while Hardy compared him with only Euler or Jacobi.

As mentioned earlier, Ramanujan had a scholarship of

250 pounds per year from the University of Madras, of which 50 pounds were allocated to support his family in India, and an exhibition of 60 pounds from Trinity. In view of the almost ludicrously simple tastes that Ramanujan had, this was plenty of money, and he was rather able to save a good amount of money which he used later. He was assigned no duties and could spend his time as he pleased. He indeed wanted to qualify for a Cambridge degree as a research student but looking at the amount of research he already had with him it was just a formality.

Ramanujan was making a great progress in his work, because for the first time in his life he was now in a real comfortable position and was able to devote his entire time in research without any anxiety. Before going to England, six papers of Ramanujan were published and on reaching England he was re-assessing and extending the results. Although, in the year 1914, Ramanujan had only one paper published, which was on "Modular Equations and Approximation of Pi", of about 25 pages and appeared in Quarterly Journal of Mathematics, but by June 1914, in just about two months of his arrival in England, he had already written two papers, as is evident in the letter he wrote to his friend R. Krishna Rao, nephew of B. Ramachandra Rao. Note that B. Ramachandra Rao had helped Ramanujan greatly by providing him a scholarship of twenty-five rupees per month. These two papers of him were presented on 11th June 1914 by G.H. Hardy in the meeting of the London Mathematical Society. In the year 1915, he of course published 9 papers including his famous paper on Highly Composite Numbers, which was about 65 pages and appeared in Proceedings of the London Mathematical Society, XIV (1915), pp. 347-409. This paper was presented by Professor Hardy in the meeting of the London Mathematical Society sometime in the late fall of 1914.

The letter that Ramanujan wrote to his friend R. Krishna Rao is produced below (see Berndt and Rankin [4], in Section 14.2 of this book).

6.4 Ramanujan to R. Krishna Rao:

11 June, 1914
Trinity College

My dear Krishna Rao,

Please excuse me for the long delay in writing to you. Now I am somewhat accustomed to the living here. Till now I did not feel comfortable and I would often think why I had come here. It is due to the difficulty of getting proper food. Had it not been for good milk and fruits here I would have suffered more. Now I have determined to cook one or two things myself and have written to my native place to send some necessary things.

After enjoying the pleasant voyage except for two or three days when I was seasick, I reached London on 14th April when Mr. Neville and his brother were kindly waiting at the docks and took me to Cromwell Road where I remained a few days. I came to Cambridge on 18th evening and remained for some days in Mr. Neville's house.

Now I am living in the college and going to stay here for the future also even though it is more costly than lodging houses, as it will be inconvenient for the professors and myself if I stay outside the college.

Mr. Hardy, Mr. Neville and others here are very unassuming, kind and obliging. As soon as I came here, Mr. Hardy paid twenty pounds to the college for my entrance and other fees and made arrangements to give me a scholarship of forty pounds a year. The remaining twenty pounds may be given in due course or may be taken for the fees of tutors.

I am attending lectures and have written two articles till now. Mr. Hardy is going to London today to read a paper on one of my results before the London Mathematical Society.

I hope you have passed your examination. Is your brother coming here?

My respects to your uncle and compliments to your brother.

Yours sincerely
S. Ramanujan
c/o G.H Hardy Esq.
Trinity College

The above letter of Ramanujan was replied by R. Krishna Rao on 7th July 1914, and in reply to that Ramanujan wrote the following letter on 7th August 1914 to R. Krishna Rao. By this time, as appears in the letter below, Ramanujan had received the proof sheets of three papers, and was in the process of writing three more papers. All these papers appeared in the year 1915 (see the book by Berndt and Rankin [4], in Section 14.2 of this book).

7 August 1914
Trinity College

My dear Krishna Rao,

Received your letter of 7th July. Very glad to hear that you have passed your apprentice examination. Glad to hear also that Mr. Ananda Rau is coming here, and I am ready to help in any sort of way I can be of use to him.

I came here at the end of the year for the climatic conditions as you know. The college was closed in the middle of June and it will be reopened in the middle of October. There is nobody here except Prof Hardy as the examinations are all over and all have gone outside. I can write to you something interesting to you after the vacation is over. That is why I have nothing to write to you at present and you will excuse me for that.

I have written three papers till now. The proof sheets have come. I am writing three more papers. All will be published at the end of the vacation, i.e., in October.

It will be difficult for Mr. Ananda Rau to reach London through the Channel and the Thames owing to the present war, and so it is better for him to get down at Plymouth or some other seaport. Has your brother determined to go over here? Hoping all in your family are doing well and wishing a happy and successful career in life.

Yours sincerely
S. Ramanujan
Trinity College
Cambridge

P.S. I am living within the college premises and am cooking my food myself though it takes so much of my time. I am getting things from a company at London selling Indian things, as well as from my home.

Yours sincerely

S. *Ramanujan*

After this Ramanujan wrote several letters to his family and friends in India and some of these letters are produced below (see Berndt and Rankin [4], in Section 14.2 of this book).

13 August 1914
Trinity College

My dear Krishna Rao,

Ananda Rau has joined King's College and settled quite comfortably. He is also coming to this college to attend some lectures.

I am attending only some of the University lectures. A few students from America and Japan have come here to attend these lectures.

I am very slowly publishing my results owing to the present war. A lecturer here whom I knew well and from whom I received some help to publish my results has gone to war. The other professors here whom I know have lost their interest in Mathematics owing to the present war. One of the professors here, some days back, remarked that I have come to England in the most unfortunate time.

I have changed my plans of publishing my results. I am not going to publish any of the old results in my notebook till the war is over. After coming here I have learned some of their methods. I am trying to get new results by their methods so that I can easily publish these results without delay.

In a week or so I am going to send a long paper to the London Mathematical Society. The results in this paper have nothing to do with those of my old results.

I have published only three short papers, two of which I have sent to your uncle. For the mathematical side you may ask Mr. Seshu Aiyar or your uncle whenever you meet them.

I don't write anything about the war, so that the letter may reach you safely.

I was silent so long as I had nothing to write to you. Hereafter I may tell you something about my progress as the professors here are somewhat receiving their lost interest in Mathematics.

As for my food I have no other go but to cook myself. There is no place very near the college where I can get vegetarian food and I can 't go out of the college. I am getting some of the Indian things here. I will be very much obliged if you can send me some tamarind (seeds being removed) and good coconut oil by postal parcel through the cheapest route. Coconut oil is the best as it will be solid owing to cold and won't be spoiled. I can use lemons instead of tamarind if they are sour; but unfortunately the lemons here are not sour like our lemons and moreover they are not properly lemons at all but they are sweet Narthangai. I can receive the things only in proper order if you send me by postal parcel, otherwise it will be very difficult for me to go London harbor to receive the things. I beg to be excused for the trouble.

Yours sincerely

S. *Ramanujan*

Commentary: The lecturer who helped Ramanujan and went to war was J.E. Littlewood.

The paper that Ramanujan submitted to the London Mathematical Society in the late fall of 1914 is his famous paper on highly composite numbers.

Tamarind is a fruit with a sour and tart taste and is used in South Indian cooking. The tamarind tree is a beautiful large shady tree with small leaves. Tamarind trees are frequently planted along the sides of roads to give welcome shade to pedestrians.

Narathangai, a tangy citrus fruit similar to grapefruit, is dried in the sun and salted. Afterward, the fruit is then stored in jars and used as a pickle for rice and yogurt.

The letter given below was written by Ramanujan to Mr. E. Vinayaka Row, who was born on 14th July 1891 at Tanjore. He attended Kumbakonam Town High School for boys and then graduated from Pachaiyappa's College in Madras (now Chennai). He was a very distinguished student in University of Madras and for some time worked as Tutor in Pachaiyappa's College. Later he studied for law in the Law College, Madras (now Chennai), and then joined the bar and practiced in Madras High Court. Ramanujan likely had contact with him when he was a student at Pachaiyappa's College. Both, Ramanujan and Vinayaka Row had mutual interest in mathematics and mathematics students and teachers of Pachaiyappa's College.

Again, this letter has been taken from the book (see Berndt and Rankin [4], in Section 14.2 of this book).

6.5 Ramanujan to E. Vinayaka Row:

11 June 1914
Trinity College

My dear Vinayaka Row,

Your kind letter to hand. Very glad to hear that Suryanarayanan has got the Scholarship. Please excuse me for the long delay in writing to you. It is because that I felt quite uncomfortable till now.
The voyage on the whole was very pleasant though I suffered from seasickness for two or three days in the Mediterranean. As soon as I arrived to England on the 14th April, Mr. Neville was kind enough to come to the docks and take me to Cromwell road. After staying a few days at London I came to Cambridge on 18th evening. But as I came here in the middle of the year I couldn't find

licensed lodging here and stayed in Mr. Neville's house for few weeks, and then came to the college.

Living in college is more costly than in lodging houses. Cambridge is a costly place, next comes Oxford (?). I have no idea of the cost. I have to pay all the expenses every term unlike the lodging houses where the expenses are paid weekly. The college pays me 40 pounds a year of which 20 pounds is given to the college for my entrance and other fees.

I am staying in the college because there will be much inconvenience to the professors and myself, if I stay outside the college. I would advise Suryanarayanan to try to live in an unlicensed lodging house, he will find it by far cheaper than other places.

As for the food I would have suffered much more had it not been for the good milk obtained here. For the first two months I felt why I had come here. Now I am alright. Suryanarayanan will also feel the same for two months from the time he comes. Let him not be discouraged it is only a matter of two months until a vegetarian will be home again. Let him select such lodgings where good vegetarian food was given previously to the Indian occupant. He can easily get information when he is coming in....

There is another Suryanarayan here who was a tutor in the Pachaiyappa's College. He says that he knows you all. He is living in a lodging where they prepare excellent food. During voyage there will be no difficulty because most of them will be Indians and he may tell them whatever he wants. Let him be prepared to take meals in an English Restaurant in Madras, for it will be very awkward in the beginning if he remains taking food in his house to the last moment. It is also better for him to cook one or two things for himself after coming here, if he cannot find a good house and if he finds time. Let him be careful not to use fried things as they will just fat and not to take things as they may contain.... After coming here he... cooks to fry things if he wants. For vegetarian... eggs it will be difficult in the beginning is no difficulty.

As for my studies, I am attending a few lectures and have begun to write articles and publish my results. I have two articles one on Definite Integrals and another on Elliptic functions. Another I am going to write soon on continued fractions. My hearty congratulations to Suryanarayanan.

Yours affectionately,

S. *Ramanujan*

As a Resident Scholar, Ramanujan was expected to reside in College. However, from the point of view of his health it was better for him to live in lodgings, especially those where the excellent vegetarian food was available.

Below is the letter that Ramanujan wrote to E. Vinayaka Row on 24th March after receiving his letter of 18th February 1915 (see Berndt and Rankin [4], in Section 14.2 of this book).

24 March 1915
Trinity College

My dear Vinayaka Row,

Received your letter of 18th Feb. I have received all your letters. It appears from your letter that you have not received my letter. In that letter I wrote you mainly about the war.

I was not well till the beginning of this term owing to the weather and consequently I couldn't publish anything for about 5 months. This term I have published 3 or 4 pamphlets and a long paper. Up to this time I have written on the following subjects.

Definite Integrals, Modular equations and approximations to π (Elliptic functions), Definite integrals (which come out in finite terms for the rational values of the parameter and not for irrational values). Series connected with the Euler's Constant, Sum of the square roots of the natural numbers (and some allied sums), New expressions for the Riemann

Zeta function. Some series having curious properties, and a very long paper on the Divisor of a number. All these are published in the 'Messenger of Mathematics' and the 'London Mathematical Journal.' Except the first 3 papers all others are being printed. Suryanarayanan is not appearing for the I.C.S. as he has a very bad short sight. He will not be selected even if he comes in the top of the list. He will enter the Educational service. I am glad to inform you that he shines in the public speech in various societies and has glorious tutorial reports in his college.

I hope you and your family are doing well and wish you success in the B.L. examination.

With best wishes

I am—Yours sincerely

S. *Ramanujan*

6.6 Ramanujan writes to his mother Komalata-Ammal:

All the letters below have been taken from the book (see Berndt and Rankin [4], in Section 14.2 of this book).

11 September 1914
Trinity College

Salutations to the great Ramanuja! Ramanujan makes his countless prostrations to his mother and writes. Please write about your welfare. The letters you write reach me regularly. The three letters written on August 4, 10 and 11 reached me. I could not write letters for two weeks. You will henceforth be getting letters every week. There is no war in this country. War is going on only in the neighbouring country. That is to say, war is waged in a country that is as far as Rangoon is away from the city (Madras). Lakhs of persons have come here from our country to join the forces. Seven hundred Rajas have come here from our country to wage war. Ultimate victory will come only to the King of this country. You need not send any provisions. Ramachandra Rao's relative Ananda Rau a youngster, has come to this country for study. He has not yet reached this place. He will come in October. Mr. Seshu Aiyar has told him to take with him numerous articles for being given to me. He and another youngster Sankara Rao have arrived in England.

When they reached the town of Port Said, the war commenced.

Unknowingly they had sailed in the enemy ship. Their intention was to travel in an Austrian ship, get down at Austria and reach here by train. But while nearing the Island of Crete on the way to Austria after leaving Port Said, the crew of the English ship fired in the air to stop the ship and know its identity. Providentially, the ship stopped as it carried no guns. If the men of the ship had also fired, the ship would have been shot and sunk. The ship was captured and all the persons in the ship were taken prisoners and carried to Alexandria and the ship was seized. The people coming from our country and the Englishmen were put in another ship and sent here. These two youngsters reached after escaping this danger.

No war like this has waged before. The present war affects crores of people. It is not one or two crores. Germans set fire to many a city, slaughter and throw away all the people, the children, the women and the old. The small country Belgium is almost destroyed. Each town has buildings fifty to hundred times more valuable than those in Madras city.

In many towns, the people of the towns themselves blow off the supports of the bridges over rivers, leave them hanging in midair, spray gunpowder all over the street, lay mine and cover them up and remain ready to flee. When enemies come, the bridges fall and half of them are carried off by the current of the river and when the rest enter the city, the dwellers themselves burn the city and flee. When streets are ablaze, the enemies try to escape but the iron wire get round their legs and they perish,

unable to run away.
War is waging at many places. Each place has an extent of 200 miles. This is on the land. Many ships are sunk by battles raging in the oceans. These are of two kinds. One is to fire directly at a ship, the other is to go under water, knock at the enemy ship and sink it. Not only this. They fly in airplanes at great heights, bomb the cities and ruin them. As soon as enemy planes are sighted in the sky, the planes resting on the ground take off and fly at great speeds and dash against them resulting in destruction and death.
All that you sent got broken but reached me without falling off because of the supporting cloth. I get everything here. I get certain provisions from the city (Madras). You need not send anything.

Yours,
Ramanujan

Commentary: One lakh equals 100,000 and one crore equals 10,000,000. The above letter was written by Ramanujan in his native language. The above letter is the English translation taken from the book by Berndt and Rankin (see [4, pp. 112-119], in Section 14.2 of this book).

The letter given below is the English translation of the letter Ramanujan wrote in his native language, Tamil, to his father on 17 November 1914. This letter has also been taken from the book by Berndt and Rankin (see [4], in Section 14.2 of this book).

6.7 Ramanujan writes to his father Srinivasa Aiyangar:

17 November 1914
Trinity College

Salutations to the great Ramanuja! Ramanujan makes his countless prostrations to his father and writes. Well and wish to hear the same from you. I got your letter. I have also received the letter written earlier by Thirunarayanan.

I have all the pickles. I get tamarind etc. from Madras. You need not send anything. Except the kuzhuvidam (dried up precooked foodstuff made of flour) which you are sending now., do not send any other thing. My college was closed last week. It is to open in the middle of January. I am getting on well. Keep the house in such a way that it is attractive to look at. Do not allow the gutter to run as usual. Pave the place with bricks and keep it well. I am getting on well. The students who have come from our place have joined the neighboring college.

Yours,
Ramanujan

Commentary:

1. Ramanujan is joking with his father about the gutter, which extended from the cooking area into the backyard and served to carry away liquid refuse from cooking.
2. Thirunarayanan was Ramanujan's youngest brother.
3. Kuzhuvidam is made from rice or tapioca and left to dry in the sun. Fried in oil, Kuzhuvidam can be prepared very quickly. It can then be stored, e.g., in jars, for a long time.

As is evident from his above letter to E. Vinayaka Row, Ramanujan was making great progress in his work, but the limitations of his knowledge were as startling as his profundity. In some ways the collaboration between Hardy and Ramanujan made an odd pair, because Hardy was a great exponent of rigorous analysis while Ramanujan arrived at his results by a process of mingled argument, intuition, and induction, of which he was not able to give any reasoning or proof. This was in fact due to the lack of formal education in Ramanujan and so it was a big challenge for Hardy to teach him without giving him any feeling of this deficiency. Hardy indeed tried his best to provide the gaps in Ramanujan's education without ever discouraging him, and was successful.

According to Hardy, on one hand Ramanujan could work out modular equations, and theorems on complex multiplication with his knowledge on continued fractions beyond that of any mathematician in the world, but on the other hand he had never heard of Cauchy's Theorem in the theory of complex variable, and in fact had virtually no idea what a function of complex variable was. Hardy used to be surprised by Ramanujan's intuition and ability in manipulating infinite series and continued fractions. Even, all the results that he had brought from India were also obtained by a process of mingled argument, intuition, and induction because of his not having an idea as to what a mathematical proof was. As a result some of his results, in particular those concerning distribution of primes, to which he attached the greatest importance were wrong. Hardy therefore had to teach him the theory of functions and the analytic theory of numbers, in which he became quite successful, although Hardy said that he learned more from Ramanujan than Ramanujan learned from him. Hardy even used to mention that he has never met Ramanujan's equal, and compared Ramanujan only with Euler or Jacobi. Ramanujan could not become a modern mathematician of his time but after studying for few years with Hardy he had developed the ability and skills to decide if the proof of a theorem he has obtained is correct or wrong.

In any case, Ramanujan's stay in Cambridge turned out to be a very successful period of collaboration between Hardy and Ramanujan. Ramanujan lived in England for five years and during these years he published extensively on a wide variety of topics, which includes the Distribution of Prime Numbers, Hypergeometric Series, Elliptic Functions, Modular Forms, Probabilistic Number Theory, The Theory of Partitions, and q-Series.

According to Hardy (see, Hardy, Aiyar and Wilson [8] in Section 14.2 of this book), Ramanujan had very little interest in literature, or in art, though he could distinguish good literature from bad. He was a keen philosopher, and adhered to the religious observances of his caste, but religion was a matter of just observance, as he had once told Hardy that to him, all religions seemed equally true.

□

7

Extension of Scholarship and University Degree to Ramanujan

As mentioned earlier, Ramanujan was granted a research scholarship of £250 per annum for two years by Madras University to work at Trinity College, Cambridge. Out of this, £50 per annum were being sent to his family. In 1915, this research scholarship awarded to Ramanujan was approaching its end of two years. The Madras University initiated steps with Trinity College to ascertain Ramanujan's progress. Towards the end of 1915, it was time for reports, recommendations and decision to arrive for extension of his scholarship.

Also, in Trinity College, the status of Ramanujan was that of a 'Research Scholar'. However, there was a problem. Ramanujan had no university degree. In his case this requirement was waived, and this needed some correction to the situation. So beside extension of the research scholarship, something needed to be done to be free from this anomaly.

7.1 Excellent Progress Report:

In Cambridge, every student was assigned a tutor who advised him on academic matters, and monitored his progress. Ramanujan's tutor was E.W. Barnes, a well-recognized mathematician. He submitted his report on Ramanujan by the following letter written to Francis Dewsbury, the Registrar of Madras University:

8 Nov., 1915

Dear Sir:
The work and progress of Mr. S. Ramanujan is excellent. He is entirely justifying the hopes entertained when he came here. There can be no doubt at all that his scholarship should be extended until, as I confidently expect, he is elected to a Fellowship at the College. Such an Election I should expect in October 1917.

Yours faithfully
E.W. Barnes
Fellow and Tutor of Trinity College

Soon after a couple of days, Hardy wrote to Dewsburry his report in which he said,

"*.......Ramanujan beyond question the best Indian mathematician of modern times... He will always be rather eccentric in his choice of subjects and methods of dealing with them. But of his extraordinary gifts there can be no question in some ways he is the most remarkable mathematician I have ever known*".

In Madras (now Chennai), Sir Francis Spring, having received following letter from Ramanujan, addressed to Mr. S. Narayana Iyer sent his support to Francis Dewsbury for an extension of two years. A similar letter on the same date was written by Ramanujan to Mr. R. Ramachandra Rao.

Trinity College, Cambridge
11th Nov., 1915

My dear Sir
Your kind letter duly to hand. Very glad to hear of the kind remembrances of Sir Francis Spring. Had it not been for his special recommendation to the Government of Madras, I would not have got the scholarship so easily and quickly from Madras University. He will be glad if he knows from you about my progress.
I am sending you one of my papers read before the London

Math. Society in last November. It is wrongly printed in the paper that it was read in last June. The paper that was read last June was about some of my results in my notebook. It will take some month for me to write that paper systematically and publish it.

As for your suggestion to publish more important and general results, I have first to read French and German works and journals and to become familiar with extremely rigorous proofs and then publish my results. Now I shall be going on to write something in my own way for 6 or 7 months to come. Unless I remain here for two years more I cannot do all I have to do. If I just consider the enormous losses to this college owing to terrible war, I have no voice to ask the authorities of the college to do me anything if they cannot afford to retain me here of their own accord. There were about 700 students and even more than that sometimes before the war; but there are only about 150 this year. Perhaps there may be very few only next year if the war continues.

It appears that Madras University has asked this college about my work. I think the reports may reach Madras very soon after you receive this letter if they have not already reached there. If I could remain here for more

than one year I should like to go over there for the coming long vacation so that I may not disappoint my people to whom I promised to return at the end of two years of my stay here.

I shall be very much obliged to you if you take so much trouble as to let Sir Francis Spring know all I have written to you. He will make all the necessary arrangements for my further stay here as well as for my voyage to India.

I am ever indebted to you and Sir Francis Spring for your zealous interest in my case from the very beginning of the acquaintance.

Yours sincerely,
S. Ramanujan

PS—I am glad to tell you that I may be conferred upon the Research Degree next month.

7.2 Awarded B.A. (honoris causa) from London University:

The University, keeping in view the possibility of getting Fellowship from Trinity, extended the current research scholarship for one year. Another characteristic of the recognition of Ramanujan's great mathematical talent and appreciation was that in March 1916 he was awarded degree of *'Bachelor of Arts, by Research'* (B.A.) (honoris causa) from London University, on the basis of his famous paper 'Highly Composite Numbers, published in the Proceedings of the London Mathematical Society XIV (1915), 347-409'. This paper was of 63 pages and is considered extraordinary. This degree, *'Bachelor of Arts, by Research'* (B.A.) (honoris causa) from London University was later renamed Ph.D.

It may be mentioned that as many as nine papers of Ramanujan appeared in 1915, and his three papers appeared in the year 1916—two in *Messenger of Mathematics* and one in the *Transactions of the Cambridge Philosophical Society.*

□

8

Ramanujan's Life in England

Moving from one country to another country, even today, when this has increased multiple times in almost all countries including India, has its challenges of adjustment, sufferings and facing prejudices. Moving from India to England that too in 1914, had its challenges for Ramanujan as well, although according to an information there were about a thousand Indian students studying in English universities there. Between the two countries, there was a big gap in culture, civilization, language, religion, and what not, all the more when India as a colony was ruled by Britain. Many a times an Indian experienced downright racial prejudice. Of the two countries, cultural characteristics differed substantially. According to the film on Mahatma Gandhi (written by John Briley and produced and directed by Richard Attenborough, with Ben Kingsley acting as Mahatma Gandhi), who went there in 1887, one can see the realistic high handedness he faced by British public and the police. Ramanujan also had to face some of the high handedness by British public and police. This certainly affected his life.

8.1 Ramanujan's problems of adjustment in England:

Ramanujan mostly stayed in his room in Whewell's Court (a five-minute walk from where Hardy lived), hardly ever going out and that to library or to the office of the Department of Mathematics.

A typical British in his disposition, by nature, does not show emotions like in USA and some other countries. For example, it is not common for a British to applause or praise after an admiring speech or show. In Cambridge, the environment was deeply personal about things, work, ideas, events, responsibilities, and games, etc. This was quite different from what Ramanujan lived with in Madras (now Chennai). For example a typical practice of Indian children paying respect to parents and elders was not in vogue in Britain.

For Ramanujan the academic environment of Cambridge was also quite different than what it was there in Madras (now Chennai). In the beginning, a British student would pass unfamiliar strange remarks to an Indian. Away from home and family, there were several factors that were important. Roughly these in nature were usually physical, mental, intellectual, etc. and in the case of Ramanujan they were also his spiritual frames arising out of his reverence for Goddess Namagiri.

Let us first reflect on Ramanujan's daily life and food arrangement. Ramanujan was raised and lived as a conservative Hindu Brahmin. He had faith in Hindu Gods and Goddesses. On the walls of his room, he had put up pictures of Hindu Gods and Goddesses. He would get up early in the morning, take bath, putting on *dhoti* (long cloth), putting sacred marks of colors and ash on his forehead, go through routines of worship, reciting mantras, doing meditation, etc. He would put on western clothes only when he would leave his hostel room for going out.

Ramanujan was a strict and orthodox Brahmin vegetarian of South Indian habits, eating only homemade food. Orthodox Brahmins are very touchy about their food caring for—what to eat, who cooks, and also where to eat. There is a group of Brahmins, in which after a certain age, for reasons of purity and for avoiding even an iota of contamination, every individual cooks food for himself. Ramanujan never cooked food in India. His mother and later his wife did it. There being no vegetarian restaurant in Cambridge, he had to do the cooking himself. In fact, that was one of the problems so resolved in convincing him to travel to Cambridge. After reaching Cambridge a couple of times he did go to the college canteen and ate fried potatoes, but then another Tamil Brahmin boy laughingly told that these are fried in lard. Thereafter, Ramanujan never took anything to eat from the college canteen. He cooked South Indian vegetarian preparations—*rice, yogurt, rasam, sambhar, dosa, idli,* etc.—normally once in a day or once in two days. Soon after arriving in Cambridge, he had written to a friend, about this.

> *".... The difficulty of getting proper food. Had it not been for the good milk and fruits here I would have suffered more. Now I have determined to cook one or two things myself, and have written to my native place to send some necessary things for it."*

He received powdered rice weekly/monthly from Narayana Iyer, while others sent him spices, pickled fruits and vegetables.

His social interaction with British was minimal, except with Hardy and other few mathematics faculty with whom he would meet more often. His shy nature, staying aloof, keeping himself busy in his research, not going out of his room in the Bishop hostel as the routine, and extraordinary reserved nature and indifference of Englishmen were some of the factors responsible for this.

Somehow, Ramanujan was also not disposed to extend a circle of British friends. This was perhaps due to the cultural and religious differences. As has been mentioned earlier Ramanujan was an orthodox Brahmin who followed his religion very strictly by offering prayers to Goddess Namagiri of Namakkal after taking bath every morning, which was not so common in England those days. Furthermore, Ramanujan did not like to waste time, and in fact had no time to spend on anything other than mathematics.

On the social level, Ramanujan perhaps did not have much interaction with Hardy also. Whenever they met, they just discussed mathematics. Of course, besides discussing mathematics, they were in deeper mutually grateful relationship of having found each other. In this connection, from the writings of Hardy, following passages may be considered giving good indications.

> *"Ramanujan was an Indian, and I suppose that it is always a little difficult for an Englishman and an Indian to understand one another properly. ....I rely, for the facts of Ramanujan's life, on Seshu Aiyar and Ramachandra Rao..... Here I must admit that I am to blame, since there is a good*

deal which we should like to know now and which I could have discovered quite easily.

I saw Ramanujan almost every day, and could have cleared up most of the obscurity by a little cross-examination. I am sorry about this now, but it does not really matter much, and it was entirely natural. He [Ramanujan] was a mathematician anxious to get on with the job. And after all I too was a mathematician, and a mathematician meeting Ramanujan had more interesting things to think about than historical research. It seemed ridiculous to worry about how he had found this or that known theorem, when he was showing me half a dozen new ones almost every day."

Apart from this, Hardy had many other responsibilities, interests and commitments. He was active in several areas of mathematics. In between 1915 and 1918, he wrote 45 papers out of which only four were with Ramanujan. He was active in 'London Mathematical Society,'and had to attend its meeting as an office bearer. He was as well associated with 'Cambridge Philosophical Society,'some other mathematical organizations and 'Trinity Essay Society'. Cricket was his favorite game and he daily played tennis.

Ramanujan (centre) and G.H. Hardy (extreme right), with other scientists, outside the Senate House, Cambridge, c.1914-1919

It is well recorded that Ramanujan had no political views or affiliations. On the other hand, Britain was engaged in the World War and Hardy had sharp views on it. His affiliates in mathematics also had quite strong views on war. Readers may be familiar with the name of Bertrand Russell, who along with being a mathematician was a well-recognized thinker and philosopher. In those years, there was quite some unrest and controversy around Russell on matters of the war, in Trinity. He was against the war, and having joined the 'Non-conscription Fellowship', he was opposing conscription promulgated by the Government. In April 1916, Mr. Everett, a school teacher, was called up for service in the non-combatant corps. On conscientious call he refused and was court-martialed with a sentence of two years with hard labor. Russell representing 'Non-Conscription Fellowship' brought out a leaflet in defense of Everett. On July 11, 1916, Russell was fired from Trinity. Hardy, Littlewood, Barnes, Neville and some other persons following Russell's line, protested and had strong anti-war views. There were other cases also in Cambridge, where Hardy had on record anti-war activities. However in many ways, Hardy was his best and trusted friend.

On a personal side, in the beginning Ramanujan was noted for his shyness and unfriendliness. However, he was a dignified man with pleasant manners. He lived a simple life at Cambridge. He was a rigorously orthodox Hindu, who credited his acumen to his family Goddess, Mahalakshmi of Namakkal and looked for her inspiration for his work. He claimed that he receives visions of scrolls of complex mathematical results before his eyes. He used to say that *"An equation for him has no meaning unless it represents a thought of God".*

8.2 Interaction with some Indian students:

Among Indian students, he had become very popular and was treated as a legendary person. His achievements were a matter of common talks and appreciation. His room was viewed as a shrine. Prasanta Chandra Mahalanobis, who later was also elected as a 'Fellow of Royal Society', was then a student at King's College. They would meet and would go for shopping and walk together.

Some others were Ananda Rau and G.C. Chatterji. C.D. Deshmukh, who after Indian independence became Finance Minister in the Government of India, in the cabinet of Pandit Jawahar Lal Nehru, reached Cambridge in 1915 for higher education and has later generously recalled Ramanujan. Ramanujan in company of Indian students was very light hearted—telling jokes, bursting in laughter, and discussing and talking of Hindu stories and philosophical topics. He was extremely well educated in Hindu religion and in general talked authoritatively about Hindu philosophies.

C.D. Deshmukh

P.C. Mahalnobis

The conditions, particularly the war, denied Ramanujan's access to mathematicians with whom he had been brought to England to work. It had undermined his nutrition, and health leading to sickness.

8.3 Ramanujan falls sick:

Due to war in England, there was shortage of consumable items. Prices had gone up by about 65 percent. Persons living there were experiencing difficulty in getting milk, butter, potatoes, sugar etc. Availability of fruits had become all the more difficult. Ramanujan who was somehow depending on milk and fruits naturally experienced greater difficulty. Scarcity of nourishing food items, irregularity of food, excessive work, social neglect, loneliness, cold weather of Cambridge, worries of all different kind were effecting his health adversely, and as a result around April 1917, he fell ill.

Initial medication being not of much help, he was admitted in a close by nursing home—a small private hospital catering to Trinity patients—not far from the residence of Neville. He became very ill. Worried Hardy sent an early message to Ramachandra Rao in India through 'Master of Trinity'. Later when the condition improved, then he wrote to Ramachandra Rao not to worry and to inform Subrahmanyan.

As a patient, it had not been easy to handle Ramanujan. He was a terrible patient. He had become obstinate; used to cry loudly in his aches and pains. He had no faith in the effectiveness of medicine and was reluctant to consume them. Initially he would place trust in the doctor, but not seeing relief, developed all distrust in him, and would request to get away from him. He, being a strict vegetarian, became very picky about the food. Perhaps he saw death approaching. Doctors in England were reluctant to take him as their patient. In sickness period of roughly two years, he entered at least five hospitals and underwent treatment of eight different doctors.

In the beginning he was suspected and treated for 'gastric ulcer'. Not being sure, an exploratory surgery was also considered. After exploring different possible ailments, he was identified with tuberculosis and was treated for that.

Tuberculosis was considered an uncurable illness then, the medicine streptomycin was yet to be discovered. For the recovery of tuberculosis patients, at distant places in natural surroundings sanatoriums were made. It was believed that in healthy surroundings, with nourishing food and complete rest, patients would be benefitted. Ramanujan had to stay in a sanatorium for a rather long period. It may be noted that Mrs. Kamala Nehru, wife of Pandit Jawahar Lal Nehru (Ex-Prime Minister of India) was also sent to live in one such sanatorium in Switzerland.

8.4 Neglected and maltreated in a British sanatorium:

Around October, 1917 he was moved to Mendip Hills Sanatorium at Hill Grove, near Wells in Somerset. There he met and was treated by Indian physician, Dr. Chowry Muthu, who by chance was known to Ramanujan, because he had traveled with Ramanujan on Nevasa ship three years earlier, while coming to England. Dr. Muthu was a tuberculosis specialist.

In the month of November, Ramanujan was moved to Matlock House Sanatorium in Derbyshire. There he was treated by at least three doctors and the expenses ran quite high. He was not happy there, as is clear from the following letter that he wrote to Hardy.

> *"I have been here a month and I have not been allowed fire even for a single day. I have been shivering from cold many a time and have not been able to take my meals sometimes. In the beginning I was told that I could not possibly have any except the welcome fire I had for an hour or two when I entered this place. After a fortnight of stay they told me that they received a letter from you about one and promised me fire on those days in which I do some serious mathematical work. That day hasn't come yet and I am left in this dreadfully cold open room".*

It may be mentioned that the staff of Matlock were putting Ramanujan to cruel treatment by not providing proper heating in his room. The facts are that in 'open air treatment'in those days a Sanatorium had instructions to open windows of the room for fresh air and better recovery from tuberculosis, there being no medicine for the disease.

The treatment for tuberculosis those days was rigorous. Patients were kept in unheated airy rooms, with only blankets to protect them from cold, because it was believed that the lungs could somehow be cleansed through fresh, cold air. Also, the food Ramanujan received at Trinity was always a problem because of the food not being cooked according to Ramanujan's pledge of maintaining a strict Hindu diet that must be prepared strictly under

Brahmin oversight, and in this case of his own since there was no Brahmin cook. Ramanujan therefore insisted for being allowed to do his own cooking but only after his Indian friends, who visited him, convinced the management of the sanatorium of this difficulty the management allowed Ramanujan to do his own cooking.

There are theories as to why Ramanujan got infected by Tuberculosis. Tuberculosis can be aggravated or even triggered by lack of vitamin D. In England, Ramanujan was always working and would work for hours at a time. Often, he would start late at night and work until dawn. He would then cook breakfast and then sleep much of the day seeing very little sunshine because he largely kept himself to his rooms. The only place outside of his rooms he visited was Hardy's rooms where he would again work with him on Mathematics problems. Also, unlike Hardy and other Fellows of Trinity College, Ramanujan had no interest in any sports and so his life was totally sedentary. Thus Ramanujan had no exposure to sunlight and it was believed that this would have contributed in getting him infected by Tuberculosis, although later findings have suggested that he might have parasitic infection affecting his liver. No one really knows what exactly he was suffering from but he had fevers, stomach pains, and many other symptoms, which unfortunately lead him to death.

Further, a 1994 analysis of Ramanujan's medical records and symptoms by Dr. A.B. Young concluded that his medical symptoms including his past relapses, fevers and hepatic conditions, were much closer to those resulting from hepatic *amoebiasis,* an illness then widespread in Madras (now Chennai), rather than tuberculosis. He had two episodes of dysentery before he left India. If not properly treated, dysentery can lie dormant for years and lead to hepatic *amoebiasis,* whose diagnosis was not at that time well established, although *amoebiasis* was treatable and an often curable disease at that time.

8.5 War & Racial Prejudices—Trinity's Fellowship denied:

Ramanujan, partly because of the wide cultural and social differences between India and England and strict vegetarian food and also because of lack of flexibility on both sides, faced rather major adjustment problems in Trinity. He did receive good academic support and appreciation from Hardy, Littlewood, Neville and as well from his tutor Barnes. He arrived there in April 1914, but only after few months clouds of World War 1 started looming in Europe, and on August 4, 1914, England declared war with Germany. War brought many disruptions and problems for Ramanujan. His health suffered, he became seriously ill. Ramanujan broke down physically. Greater problems were awaiting. Something broke him down mentally and emotionally. He attempted suicide. It happened due to a failed attempt to honor him with a Fellowship of Trinity College, and the roots of this can be seen in following letters.

First mention of award of fellowship of Trinity College was made by Ramanujan's tutor, E.W. Barnes in the following letter he wrote in order to provide his report in November 1915 to the Registrar of Madras University, highlighting his performance. This letter has been referred elsewhere also, while discussing the extension of Ramanujan's scholarship.

8 November, 1915

To Francis Dewsbury
Registrar, Madras University

Dear Sir
The work and progress of Mr. S. Ramanujan is excellent. He is entirely justifying the hopes entertained when he came here. There can be no doubt at all that his scholarship should be extended until, as I confidently expect he is elected to a Fellowship at the College. Such an election I should expect in October 1917.

Yours faithfully

E.W. Barnes

Fellow and Tutor of Trinity College

Also on Nov. 11, 1915, Ramanujan wrote in separate letters to S. Narayana Iyer and R. Ramachandra Rao, that "I am glad to tell you that I may be conferred upon the Research Degree next March". As mentioned earlier, Ramanujan in March 1916 was conferred the B.A. degree by research which was later renamed Ph.D.

In October 1917, with war in vogue, Ramanujan was moved to Matlock Sanatorium and during that time, due to Bertrand Russell's dismissal and for his views opposing war, Hardy was in the camp opposed to Government policies.

Also in October 1917, unfortunately on racial considerations with a clear mention of Ramanujan being a black, his case was turned down as a Fellow of Trinity College. This greatly disappointed Ramanujan. He lost enthusiasm. His creativity in mathematics came to near stop, and he landed in the state of total imbalance.

8.6 Depression, Suicide attempt and election as Fellow of Royal Society:

This state of his mind was well known to Hardy. He wanted to do something to bring him out of this state of malice. To boost Ramanujan he made efforts to win some positions of academic recognitions. With his efforts on 6th December 1917, Ramanujan was elected in *London Mathematical Society.* This was a matter of some pride but not much; Ramanujan and his friends including Hardy were not quite satisfied with this.

Hardy now began efforts to get Ramanujan elected as a Fellow of *'Royal Society of London'*, an eminent scientific society of England, because he believed that selection of Ramanujan as a Fellow of the Royal Society was necessary to boost his spirit, of which Nobel Laureate of 1906, Sir J.J. Thomson, discoverer of electron was at that time President. On December 18, 1917 Ramanujan's application form was submitted to the Royal Society. Hardy proposed his name and was seconded by P.A. McMohan, and eleven other mathematicians who signed the form were N.R. Forsyth, A.N. Whitehead, E.T. Whittaker, W.H. Young, J.H. Grace, Joseph Larmour, T.J. Bromwich, E.W. Hobson, H.F. Baker, J.E. Littlewood and J.W. Nicholson. In the application, it was written that Ramanujan, a research student in mathematics, distinguished as a pure mathematician, be elected as a Fellow of 'Royal Society'. Among the signatories, all except McMohan were Wranglers of Cambridge Mathematical Tripos.

Ramanujan's deteriorating health was a matter of great concern for Hardy, so he wasted no time in convincing the high-ranking persons of the Royal Society about Ramanujan's talent. He even communicated in detail the information about Ramanujan to the then President Sir J.J. Thomson, a well-known physicist. He even mentioned in his letter that due to poor health of Ramanujan, if his selection is delayed even by one year then *"the Society will have to live forever with its failure to honor him"*. Following is the letter that Hardy submitted to Sir J.J. Thomson, the President of the Society.

> *"If he had not been ill I would have deferred him up a year or so, not that there is any question of the strength of his claim, but surely to let things take their ordinary course. As it is, I felt no time must be lost. I am nervous about trying to rush him, and I am aware that for the time being I am not an ideal supporter. And I realize that the R.S. has many other things to consider. But there is no doubt that (especially after his disappointment in the Fellowships) any striking recognition now might be a tremendous thing for him. I would make him feel that he was a success, and that it was worthwhile going on trying. It is this much more than the fear of the R. S. losing him entirely which seems to me important.*
>
> *I write on the hypothesis that his claims are such as, in the long run in any case, his case could not be denied. This is to me quite obvious. There is an absolute gulf between him and all other mathematical candidates".*

On 24th January, 1918, this proposal was considered in a meeting of the Society along with 103 other names. Hardy, Littlewood and some others were quite convinced that Ramanujan deserved the honor. But since he was being nominated for the first time, and most of the times, a Fellowship was not awarded on first time nomination, so in that sense his case was premature. Hardy's efforts culminated and in the meeting of the Royal Society held on 28th February 1918, out of 104 proposed candidates only 15 were accorded Fellowship of the Royal Society, and Ramanujan was one of them.

Ramanujan, just 31 years old, became the youngest Fellow in the history of the Royal Society, and second Indian to get this honor. Way back in 1841, Ardaseer Cursetjee, a shipbuilder and engineer was the first Indian to have the honor of being elected as a Fellow of the Royal Society.

A little earlier in January 1918, after Ramanujan got the shock of being denied Fellowship of Trinity, and his case for Fellowship was under consideration by Royal Society, he came to London from Matlock one day. He was in a high state of depression. Life seemed burden to him. He decided to commit suicide. He went to railway station and seeing a train coming his side a short distance away, jumped before it. Miraculously, the driver saw this happening and pulled the stop switch. The train with a screeching stopped a few feet before him, blood oozing from his body, hurt from the fall.

Police did make a quick investigation, and after finding that he is an eminent mathematician, they let him go, saying, "We did not want to spoil his life".

Also, there is an interesting story to support this incidence, which goes like this.

One day in 1936, about 16 years after Ramanujan's death, immersed in thoughts and unaware of the surroundings, Professor G.H. Hardy was taking a stroll along the Piccadilly Circus in London. In a flush of a second, Hardy hurriedly jumped on to the road, oblivious of a speeding motorcycle and as a result he was hit, dragged along and bruised.

Police arrived and took Hardy to Scotland Yard to record his statement where he admitted his mistake and thus absolving the motorcyclist. When Hardy was to leave the police station, a police messenger arrived and asked "Sir, are you Professor G.H. Hardy, Professor of Mathematics at the Cambridge University?"

Hardy replied 'yes'indeed, but he was perplexed. On this the messenger asked Hardy to come with him to his superior officer, who would like to talk to him. Hardy accompanied the police man and entered the office of the officer. The officer said "Professor Hardy, I have been waiting to see you for many years. In fact, I have been waiting for this occasion for 17 years, to be precise".

Hardy was dumbstruck. He thought that he could be one of his student or parent of one of his students, but could not place him.

The police officer continued, telling that he has evidence in his files to arrest Hardy for making a false statement to the police. This made Hardy not only confused but also scared, and told the officer that he is a professor of mathematics at Cambridge University and has committed no crime, and that the officer is mistaking him for someone else. On this the police officer replied "Do you remember, Professor Hardy, in February 1918 we had arrested an Indian mathematician for attempting to suicide, and he was about to commit suicide by falling before the train in an underground tube". The police officer continued that I was in charge of the case and that you arrived to give evidence.

This made Hardy remember the incident many years ago, when Ramanujan was suffering from depression, although productive in his mathematical discoveries but was ill, and not eating much. In this state of dejection, Ramanujan had tried to jump before an underground suburban train. Fortunately, the driver hit the break in time so Ramanujan was saved and escaped with some injuries.

It may be noted that this incident had happened around the time Hardy proposed Ramanujan's name for election to the Fellowship of the Royal Society. On getting the news of his arrest in the Scotland Yard, Hardy rushed to the spot. Hardy, commanding the stature of a Cambridge academic faculty and personality, informed the police that Ramanujan, a distinguished mathematician and a Fellow of the Royal Society cannot be arrested without the permission of the Crown. In reality, Ramanujan was at that time neither a Fellow of the Royal Society, and nor this was true that a Fellow of the Royal Society could not be arrested for a crime without the permission of the Crown. In fact, Hardy knowingly told these two lies fearing that if the society members come to know of the attempted suicide, some of them may suspect lunacy and block his election.

The police officer continued saying that we released him and you might have perhaps thought that you had bluffed us, but that was not the case. We had inquired and found that the man whom we had arrested was indeed a great and reputed mathematician who had lots of promise. We also knew that he was not a Fellow of the Royal Society nor there was there any prerogative that a Fellow of the Royal Society cannot be arrested without the permission of the Crown. The officer continued that I had been waiting for an occasion to let you know that we were not fooled, but we at Scotland Yard did not wish to spoil the career of this Indian mathematician. As mentioned earlier, on 28th February 1918, just few weeks after this incident, Ramanujan was elected as a Fellow of the Royal Society.

All these inevitably imply that none other than Hardy should be regarded as the foremost mentor of Ramanujan.

After being awarded Fellowship of Royal Society, Ramanujan thanked Hardy by writing,

> *"My words are not adequate to express my thanks to you. I did not even dream of the possibility of my election".*

The news reached India and on 22nd March, 1918, after which, the following letter followed:

22 March, 1918

To G.H. Hardy Esq. M.A.,
FRS, Cayley Lecturer
Cambridge University

Sir,
We have the honor to convey to you by direction, the grateful thanks of the Madras Members of the Indian Mathematical Society and the Mathematical Associations of the Presidency and Christian Colleges Madras for the aid and guidance you have been providing to Mr. S. Ramanujan in his work. A copy of the minutes of the meeting conveyed for the purposes herein enclosed.
We have the honor to be, Sir Your most obedient servants

P.V Seshu Aiyar, Representative of the Madras section of the Indian Math. Society
R. Ramanaiah, Secretary, Mathematical Association, Presidency College
L.V. Subramanian, Secretary, Mathematical Association, Christian College
P.S. May I also add my personal thanks to you for the parental care you have been bestowing on him during these months when his health has not been good?
P.V. Seshu Aiyar

After a major setback, failed suicide attempt and high recognition of becoming a F.R.S., Ramanujan's condition had started improving.

8.7 Honors and improving health:

Award of Fellowship by Royal Society, was a big moral and energy booster for Ramanujan. There were signs of all round improvements. Food at Matlock was a serious problem for Ramanujan's physical recovery. Failed suicide attempt indicated his terrible mental state and physical sufferings. Hardy feared and did express of Ramanujan's chance of not surviving for long. He had become very fussy about contents, preparation and taste of food. Neville later mentioned, "I have known him asking with unaffected apologies if he might make meal of bread and jam because the vegetables offered to him were novel and unpalatable".

A forgotten friend, A.S. Ramalingam, an engineer, whom he had met on the boat from India having heard of Ramanujan's F.R.S. award, visited him at Matlock. He was horrified by the terribly weak health of Ramanujan, and wrote a long letter to Hardy, saying in between

> *"I am shocked and horrified to find him in the thin, weak and emaciated state I have found him in.... It is with regard to food that I have to write somewhat harshly and tersely and at a good length".*

Ramalingam advised Ramanujan to be reasonable and not to be stubborn with tangible effect. He did try to arrange for a rather regular supply of South Indian food for him. Knowing that, there is better possibility of finding some Indian food in London than in Matlock, Ramanujan moved from Matlock to London and started living in Fitzroy House. Also, in research, the number of new results and theorems increased. Health showed substantial improvement. High temperature came infrequently and bodily pain were continuing. Doctors were not unanimous in finding the cause of pain, so much so that when there came up a tooth extraction, some doctors diagnosed that to be the cause of pain in the body.

Sometime during August—September 1918, Ramanujan's name was freshly proposed for award of Trinity's Fellowship. This was done by Littlewood, instead of Hardy, the reason being that Hardy was considered as one strongly biased in favor of Ramanujan. The candidature was opposed to it on two grounds. One was purely racial—a person, as Littlewood said later, "went about openly saying that he wasn't going to have a black man as Fellow", but Littlewood played a leading role in nullifying the racial issues raised against Ramanujan. Ramanujan's suicide attempt was also brought up by opponents. Attempted suicide incident was put as Ramanujan's serious unsound mental state. Littlewood then presented certificates of two medical doctors of Ramanujan being mentally healthy.

Littlewood has written afterwards that the objections raised by the opponents were ignored by the seasoned members of the Election Committee. The matter was considered on merit of the case. Being an F.R.S. was the sure strong consideration. The main argument placed in favor of Ramanujan was, "For a Fellow of Royal Society to be denied Trinity Fellowship would be a scandal", and Littlewood told his friend Herman, who was opposing, "You could not deny Trinity Fellowship to a Fellow of the Royal Society". In this connection, Herman replied, "Yes, we thought those who proposed played a dirty trick". On Thursday, 10th October, 1918, Ramanujan was elected as Fellow of Trinity.

All these honors encouraged Ramanujan in his mathematical

research, and these awards in fact acted as great incentives to Ramanujan who later continued discovering some of the most beautiful results in mathematics.

From Fitzroy House, Ramanujan wrote two letters to Hardy thereafter, in which after initial thanks etc., he mentioned about his illness in one letter and in the other letter a research problem on exhaustively considering about congruency of number theoretic function $p(\mathrm{n})$.

The first letter began with,

> *"My heartfelt thanks for your kind telegram. After you succeeded in getting me elected by the Royal Society my election at Trinity probably became very much less difficult this year".*

The second letter started with.

> *"Please tell Mr. Littlewood and Major MacMahon that I thank them very much. Had it not been for your pains and their encouragement I would be neither the fellow of the one nor that of the other".*

By looking at the results mentioned in the letter, Hardy had gathered that getting the awards, Ramanujan's intellect and creativity was booming again. His one paper, *"Some Properties of p(n), the Number of Partitions of n"* later appeared in '*Proceedings of the Cambridge Philosophical Society*', Volume of 1919.

In fact, soon after that, his another research paper, '*Proof of Certain Identities in Combinatorial Analysis*' also appeared in '*Proceedings of the Cambridge Philosophical Society*', Volume of 1919.

Both these papers were presented on 28th October, 1918 in the annual meeting of the 'Cambridge Philosophical Society'.

Right then, war took a different turn. Bolshevik Revolution led to surrender of the Russian armies to Germans. Germany withdrawing its forces from the eastern front, rushed them across central Europe towards Paris. Once again, German forces like in 1914 reached near Paris. But there was a difference. Now about a million American army persons had reached France. Germans exhausted by prolonged war could not continue and called for truce. On November 11, 1918, the war ended.

Just after two weeks, on 26th November, 1918, Hardy wrote a rather long letter to the Registrar of Madras University, Francis Dewsbury, about Ramanujan's return to India, with first and last paragraphs as follows:

> *"I have been meaning for some days to write to you again about Ramanujan. But have been prevented by stress of work. I think it is now time that the question of his temporary return to India and of his future, generally, should be considered".*

> *"He will return to India with a scientific standing and reputation such as no Indian has enjoyed before, and I am confident that India will regard him as the treasure he is. His natural simplicity and modesty has never been affected in the least by success—indeed all that is wanted is to get him to realize that he really is a success".*

□

9

Preparing to Return and Arrival in India

9.1 Grateful man of great achievements:

During four years of stay at Trinity, Ramanujan had published twenty very significant research papers. He was a recipient of the distinguished award of Fellowship of Royal Society, and so F.R.S. was appended to his name. Also, he had been awarded Fellowship at Trinity College. He had a handsome research scholarship, £250 from Madras University, which in December 1918 was extended for next six years. Additionally he was receiving £60 from Trinity. These were, by any standard, his extraordinary achievements. Also, in spite of the emotional and physical strain, Ramanujan lived his intellectual life with great zest in the company of eminent mathematicians at Cambridge. In total, his scholarship amount was substantial. There was a rare human aspect of his personality, which shows him a man of Brahmin values—one of which being spend money only as much as you need. He had not forgotten the value of money. When his scholarship money ended after failing in FA exam, he had to quit studies and had to drop out and his sustenance had to depend on the monetary support of Ramachandra Rao and tuitions. He was a kind hearted person and on receipt of extension of £250 scholarship that he was going to get in India, on January 11, 1919, he wrote the following letter to Mr. Dewsbury:

11 January, 1919

Colinette House,
2 Colinette Road,
Putney, SW 15

To the Registrar of the University of Madras:

Sir,
I beg to acknowledge the receipt of your letter of 9th December 1918, and gratefully accept the very generous help which the University offers me.
I feel, however, that after my return to India, which I expect to happen as soon as arrangements can be made, the total amount of money to which I shall be entitled will be much more than I shall require. I should hope that after my expenses in England have been paid, £50 a year will be paid to my parents and that the surplus, after my necessary expenses are met, should be used for some educational purpose, such in particular as the reduction of school-fees for poor boys and orphans and provision of books in schools. No doubt it will be possible, to make an arrangement about this after my return.
I feel very sorry that, as I have not been well, I have not been able to do so much mathematics during the last two years as before. I hope that I shall soon be able to do more and will certainly do my best to deserve the help that has been given to me.

I beg to remain, Sir

Your most obedient servant

S. Ramanujan

On the other side, he was continuously under-nourished, not physically well, suffering with a rather incurable disease, tuberculosis. Certainly there were signs of recovery in health, but the recovery could not be taken for granted. His biographer, Mr. Seshu Aiyar, has written that,

"Mr. Ramanujan's disease had assumed serious proportions by Christmas 1918, and caused such grave anxiety to his doctors in England, that, hoping to do him good, they advised him to return to his native home in India".

Around that time Ramanujan moved from Fitzroy Square to Colinette House, a nursing home in the Putney suburb on the south bank of Thames. In comparison to Matlock, this was easily accessible for visitors and friends. In fact, Ramanujan's incident of the famous 'Taxi Cab Number,' 1729, the details of which would be discussed later in Chapter 12, occurred here during Hardy's visit to Ramanujan while staying in this room.

Quite important in addition to things mentioned above, was the fact that the war was called off. India then being under British rule, there were effects of the European War on India. In fact, soon after the declaration of the war, German cruiser EMDEN struck and destroyed merchant ships in the Indian Ocean. British positions were strategically attacked by Germany not far from Madras (now Chennai) also. That created terror in Madras (now Chennai), and some people, fearful of EMDEN's attack, had fled also. Now, with war called off, there were no chances of Ramanujan having any untoward attacks and accidents in sea travel.

In his letter of November 26, Hardy had written to Dewsbury, *"I think it is now time that the question of his temporary return to India and of his future, generally, should be considered"*. This set the ball rolling for preparing to return.

On Monday, February 24, his passport formalities were completed with following entries:

Name–Srinivasa Ramanujan Aiyangar

Father's name–Mr. Srinivasa Aiyangar of Kumbakonam, Tanjore

Age–30

Profession–Research Scholar

Place and date of birth–Erode, India, 22 December 1887

Height–5 feet 6 inches

Forehead–Medium, *Eyes*–Normal, dark

Nose–Broad, *Mouth*–Normal

Chin–Normal
Color of Hair–Black
Complexion–Olive, *Face*–Oval
Any special peculiarities–Smallpox marks
National Status–British-India born, *Subject*–Hindu Brahmin.

The picture on the passport was that of an ill, thinner Ramanujan not of Ramanujan his friends knew back in India. It was also not of Ramanujan that Hardy and Littlewood saw in 1914. This is the picture widely used for him in almost all places. Some four pictures of Ramanujan have survived.

As mentioned earlier, his two papers, '*Some properties of p(n), the number of partitions of n*' and '*Congruence Properties of Partitions*' appeared in the Proceedings of the Cambridge Philosophical Society on 13 March, 1919.

In preparation to return, Ramanujan left his notebooks and lots of papers with Hardy. To carry with him, he packed a big leather suitcase with papers and books, along with a box of raisins for his two younger brothers. He was all ready to go. On March 13, 1919, Ramanujan boarded the Pacific and Orient Lines ship S.S. Nagoya.

Back in India, Ramanujan had become famous as a young mathematician—a magical genius with miraculous God gifted powers. The Mathematical Society of India met in Bombay for its second conference about ten weeks before Ramanujan's arrival in India. They all spoke of Ramanujan's great achievements. Also in Indian newspapers, particularly in Madras (now Chennai), there were write-ups about Ramanujan and of his returning to India after various grand successes. A week before his arrival Madras University registrar released a write-up about Ramanujan that appeared in all local papers.

9.2 Landed in India—back with family in India:

On March 27, 1919, Nagoya landed at Bombay Shipyard. His mother, Komalata-ammal and brother, Lakshmi Narasimhan, were there to receive him. Ramanujan, stepping out and instantly after seeing mother and brother looked around and in a tense voice exclaimed, "Where is she?" He was asking about his wife, Janaki! Mother rather angrily retorted, "Do not be vexed about her! She will come too". Ramanujan already had idea of ongoing tension between Janaki and his mother. In this respect, he has been holding that his mother has been maltreating his wife. Not finding Janaki, the enthusiasm and joy of meeting at arrival with his close people was considerably dampened.

Unfortunately, after about two years of Ramanujan's going abroad, there had built up tension between mother Komalata-ammal and wife Janaki. Janaki had gone to her brother's place and has been living away there. On arrival now, Ramanujan could not find out where Janaki was, whether at her father's place in Rajendram, with her sister in Madras (now Chennai) or with her brother in Karachi. The reality was that Janaki was not informed of Ramanujan's returning to India. However by news in papers, she had idea about it, but under the spell of an unknown fear, she could not gather the courage of reaching Bombay.

Immediately, brother, Lakshmi Narasimhan wrote letters to two-three addresses informing Janaki of Ramanujan's arrival, and that he was anxious to meet her. That was enough for Janaki and her father's family to meet him in Madras (now Chennai). She set out for Madras (now Chennai) with her brother.

9.3 Brahminic purification—from impurity of foreign land:

Ramanujan and his mother, as orthodox Brahmins, were worried about yet another matter-cleaning the social contamination incurred by going to a foreign country and traveling overseas. Purification ceremony needed to be performed for this. This purification ceremony could only be done, in his case, at the sacred temple in Rameshwaram. For social and emotional satisfaction, his mother had high priority for this soon after his arrival. But Ramanujan was physically weak and sick, and looking at his physical conditions, unfortunately for the family, this had to be skipped. Ramanujan, his mother and Lakshmi Narasimhan, took train and reached Madras (now Chennai) on April 2, 1919.

There again, not finding Janaki, he asked, "No Janaki still. Why?" Just to quieten, the mother responded, "Her father was ill, she was there, and is coming".

Going from railway station to home he reflected on having his time there some four five years back. On reaching home his old friend, Viswanatha Sastri and other close friends came to meet him and were shocked at his condition. Back home he was, of course, fondly eating South Indian dishes.

From his home, he moved to a more comfortable address—Venkata Vilas on Luz Church Road. There Sir Francis Spring, Narayana Iyer, Ramachandra Rao and many other respected persons—intellectuals, scholars, high-born Brahmins, lawyers—came to see him and offered all sorts of help and support, feeling proud of a South Indian genius leaving his mark on Britishers. On April 6, 1919, Janaki and her brother came. They were followed by her father, grandmother and younger brother from Kumbakonam.

There is a tale about the relations between Ramanujan's wife Janaki and his mother. On seeing Janaki, Ramanujan miffed at Janaki, and rebuked her. "I wrote so many letters, at times once every week, but you chose not to reply even once". On this Janaki told him that she was writing letters frequently even when she was not receiving from Ramanujan. She was handing over letters to her mother-in-law for posting, as she had no money for postage. Both of them then realized the dirty game that had been played by Ramanujan's mother, who had been hiding letters from Ramanujan and his wife Janaki.

For three months as they stayed there Janaki took care of Ramanujan. In illness, he had become harsh, bitter and impatient, at times yelling on her and his brother on slight matters. During this year the family changed residence several times.

Ramanujan wrote to the Registrar of Madras University, Francis Dewsbury on 24th April requesting him for the details of expenses on his coming back to India, and to kindly send him every month the scholarship money.

He was appointed a Professor at the University, which he accepted and wrote that he would join soon after his health improves.

□

10

Fast Deteriorating Health

Ramanujan arrived in India as a sick person. British doctors had diagnosed him with tuberculosis. For about thirteen months, living with his wife, mother, father, two brothers and grand-mother after return, he continued to struggle with his disease and failing health. He continued in this state for 13 months; often in pain; often in despair; struggling with life but still struggling to give definitive shape to new mathematical results and theories he was conceiving even in this state of illness.

The University arranged a house for him on East Agraharam Street not far from University Registrar's office. There came a time when Janaki started getting more favorable attention and closeness with Ramanujan. This particularly happened on a festival called *Shravani*—the full moon day of the Hindu calendar month '*Shravan*'. In Hinduism, there are several festivals, some every month also. Four of these are the major ones—*Shravani, Dussehra, Deepavali and Holi.* Every Hindu enthusiastically celebrates these festivals without any kind of caste restrictions, but these four festivals have special place respectively for Brahmins, Kshatriyas, Vaishyas and the others. On this Shravani day, Brahmins take ceremonial bath preferably in a river, solemnly do the *Havans* and change their *yajnopavita,* the sacred thread. A popular form of the festival widely observed by all Hindus is that sisters tie the knot of long-life on brothers'wrist and brothers will assure of their help and protection with a token gift of money.

10.1 Care and closeness received from wife, Janaki:

After having come to know of the harshness of his mother towards Janaki, Ramanujan had started taking her side on any issue or dispute. However, she was object of his short temper and rough behavior. Though while in good mood and in company of Janaki alone, he would fondly talk to her of his experiences in England, and would say, "If you were with me in England, I would not have had become ill".

Janaki, Ramanujan's wife

On August 11, 1919 was the *Shravani* festival. Ramanujan was going to take bath in the river and Janaki wanted to join him. Somehow, mother Komalata-ammal said 'No'for Janaki, while Ramanujan said 'Yes'. Siding with Janaki, Ramanujan rebelled against his mother and insisted on 'Yes'. Respectfully but assertively he told to his mother, "Janaki will go with me". To Janaki, he said many times, "If only you had gone with me to England I would not have fallen ill". There are other events and actions also that show how he treated Janaki lovingly keeping in mind the hostile behavior of his mother towards Janaki during his England period. Also Janaki fully and devotedly served Ramanujan in giving medicines, care and comfort etc. Their conversations were mostly limited to Ramanujan engagingly talking to her of things of England.

Under sufferings, unbearable pain with no improvement in health, Ramanujan had grown greatly depressed. He had become bitter and sour. Janaki, though loving and caring, was the object of his wrath, anger and impatience also. At times, he would yell at his brothers for little lapses and minor offences. He had become tired of meeting different physicians, their reports and medicines. Like in the past at Cambridge, he was not cooperative with his doctors. He would throw away medicines, break the thermometer and would show temper with family members and others.

After staying in Kodumudi for two months, Ramanujan with family, moved to Kumbakonam, a place where he spent his early years. His tuberculosis fever was there and taking its toll. Old friends—Sarangapani, Balakrishnan Iyer, Radhakrishna, and Ramachandra Rao and also their family members used to visit him regularly. In India, as in England, over a period of about nine months, he was treated by many doctors for variety of diagnoses and underwent many examinations, but his condition did not improve. In fact, he became a bundle of bones and grew gradually worse. In his letter dated 22 December 1919, the Registrar of Madras University, Francis Dewsbury wrote to Hardy,

> *"He is still in very bad health and difficult to deal with, living up in country with his family. Mr. Ramachandra Rao is doing what he can for him, but Mr. Ramanujan himself will not consent to live in a suitable environment under proper treatment. It is a great pity".*

On the whole, in the first nine months after his arrival, he changed his residence six times. He had become whimsical. Name of the first house was 'Crynant,'that sounded to him as one for crying—not with good feelings. From there he was moved to one good sounding, named 'Gometra'. He, it was reported, had refused to be treated as well. In fact, it appeared that he had given up the will to live.

10.2 Profound research during illness:

Ramanujan had grown very weak—just skin and bones. He had constantly been suffering from tuberculosis fever, and bodily pain. He was greatly troubled by repeated cough and mucus. To his friend Sarangapani, he once had said, *"I have a friend who does not leave my company even for a short while. It is the fever of my tuberculosis".*

He had got used to drinking coffee, while earlier he did not even touched it. He had difficulty in talking to his family members and friends. Every one was hurt by his harsh words and violent behavior. Before going to England, he only had nominal relationship with his wife, always doing mathematics then, but now she was all the time busy in taking care of him. Ramanujan had become greatly dependent on her.

Perhaps there were other reasons also of his rough behavior and anger. He perhaps had sensed the end of life coming near. Many research problems used to strike his mind and he wanted to jot them down. Mentally, he was always continuously occupied with new mathematical formulas and results. In fact, wife Janaki would give him slates after cleaning for working mathematics on them. He would write the results on blank papers that were put in a leather bag.

When tired of working on slates, he would lie down and at times would abruptly get up to write again. During his illness, he came up with new researches, very profound. He discovered a new class of functions that is known as 'Ramanujan's Mock Theta Functions'.

In this regard, on Jan 12, 1920 after a long gap of time, he wrote the following letter to Professor Hardy:

Dear Hardy,

"I am extremely sorry for not writing you a single letter up to now. I discovered very interesting functions recently which I call 'Mock-theta functions'. Unlike the 'False theta functions' (partially studied by Rogers) they enter into mathematics as beautifully as the ordinary theta functions. I am sending you with this letter some examples".

Ramanujan, January 12, 1920.

This letter has become a celebrated one, not only because of the tragic circumstances under which it was written, but also because it was mathematically mysterious and intriguing. In this, Ramanujan gives no definition of mock theta functions but only a list of 17 examples and a qualitative description of the key property that he noticed, like for example that these functions have asymptotic expansions.

In the letter, he sent 4 examples of Mock-theta functions of order three, 10 examples of order 5, and 3 examples of order 7. Ramanujan's this work is very highly rated. It was greatly appreciated by Hardy and he considered the letter important like the one he received from Ramanujan some seven years earlier. It had an impact on several branches of mathematics including number theory and mathematical physics.

Prof. G.N. Watson proved most of the assertions in the last letter of Ramanujan. Sixteen years after Ramanujan's death, Watson's Presidential address to London Mathematical Society was on Ramanujan's 'Mock-theta-functions'. He had remarked, "Like his other prime researches done earlier, Ramanujan will be long remembered for his 'Mock-theta functions'". Some subtle questions were raised by Watson, these questions made Mock theta functions more significant in the context of Lost Notebook discovered later. He wrote:

"Ramanujan's discovery of the mock-theta functions makes it obvious that his skill and ingenuity did not desert him at the oncoming of his untimely end. As much as any of his earlier work, the mock-theta functions are achievements sufficient to cause his name to be held in lasting remembrance".

'Mock-theta functions'are considered Ramanujan's last major discoveries. During this period, the work done by him on Mock Theta Functions' is very extensive. In all, there are some 650 formulas on them in the 'Lost Notebook'of Ramanujan. Describing his last days, Prof Seshu Aiyar has written,

> *"His no other work is so precious and product of intuition than what he discovered last days of illness. Certainly, his physical body was no doubt, failing, but his intellectual power grew proportionately keener and brighter".*

Dr. A. Selberg examined the behavior of the seventh order mock theta function near the unit circle. Professor George E. Andrews, who is considered an authority on Ramanujan's work, after taking up their studies some fifty years later found them rich, surprising and challenging. On solution of a small group of five of them, he remarked, "the first one took me fifteen minutes to prove, the second an hour. The fourth followed from the second. The third and fifth took me three months".

Ramanujan's Mock Theta Functions are not merely of theoretical importance to mathematicians, but these have been used in other disciplines also. In November 1988, in the conference of 'American Physical Society' held in Raleigh, North Carolina, USA, a paper with title *"A Study of Saltine Switching in Malignancy and Proliferation of... Using Ramanujan's Mock-Theta Function"* was presented. This indicates that these functions help in understanding cancer.

These enigmatic mock theta functions are of great relevance to both physicists and mathematicians. These functions, in particular, were studied by the Japanese physicists Tohru Eguchi, Hirosi Ooguri, and Yuji Tachikawa and the Canadian mathematician Terry Gannon. Building on the work of these mathematicians, Miranda Cheng from the University of Amsterdam, John Duncan from Case Reserve University, and Jeff Harvey from the University of Chicago formulated in 2010, a conjecture that predicted a very deep and precise relationship between Ramanujan's Mock Theta Functions and *string theory,* a hot item in theoretical physics.

The conjecture, which they called the *umbra moonshine*

conjecture, was formulated in order to place a British mathematician from Berkley, Richard Borcherd's 1992 proof in wider context of the so called *moonshine conjecture,* for which he received the Fields medal in 1998. If *umbral moonshine conjecture* is proved correct, Borcherd's work would be the first of many different *moonshine theories.* Mathematical physicists are realizing that such theories are important in string theory, which aims to answer a fundamental question, as to *what is the universe made of.*

In the joint work, Ken Ono from University of Virginia with John Duncan and Ken Ono's Ph.D. student Michael Griffin, proved on this *umbral moonshine conjecture,* a result which has placed the mathematics in the Ramanujan's deathbed letter at the front and center in cutting-edge of mathematical physics. Also, they have proved that the mock theta functions which Ramanujan conjured in the last months of his life encode astonishing symmetries in mathematics, and it is now predicted by the experts that Ramanujan's Mock Theta Functions will be found useful in the study of black holes, quantum gravity, and other theories. This accomplishment of proving *umbral moonshine conjecture* was selected for being among the top 100 stories in *Discover* magazine, in 2015.

10.3 Difficult time for the family:

All family members, ever after Ramanujan return from England were constantly worried about Ramanujan's health and life. In his last days, he was living with his family rather very simply in the bungalow with little furniture. His bed consisted of a mattress and a pillow laid on the bare floor. He had difficulty in moving around, his younger brother Thirunarayanan later recalled of his carrying him on his shoulder whenever moving from one place to another, as it had become unavoidable.

Janaki recalled that though sullen and angry most of the time, he enjoyed talking to her cracking jokes, full of wit and humor. Lying on the bed, mostly in semi-sleep position he will look at the visitors, avoid talking to them. The visitors also would silently move around without disturbing him.

Devoid of the hope of his survival, not seeing any result of medicines, the family observed some religious routines of astrological predictions. Ramanujan, who as a practicing Brahmin had also interest in astrological readings, and on earlier occasions had read his own horoscope. His own past predictions were of a life of thirty-years only. Mother, herself was also good astrologer and keenly interested in astrological readings. Around March 1920, she happened to meet a celebrated astrologer, G.V. Narayanswamy. Without introducing things much, she spoke to the astrologer for possible astrological readings about a person. Narayanswamy asked for the horoscope of the person. Komalata-ammal gave all the details from memory. After studying the horoscope Narayanswamy said, "Two things can be said about this person–*He would either become world famous and will die at the peak of his reputation or one with long life and obscure*".

Narayanswamy, having not known Ramanujan then asked, "Who is this gentleman? What is his name?" Komalata-ammal in tears said, "It is Ramanujan, I had also drawn the same predictions about him".

"Ramanujan!, I am sorry for the harsh predictions. Please do not convey to any of his relatives".

She replied, "Sir, I am the mother of this person".

Thinking of revising and softening his prediction on astrological basis, Narayanswamy, said, "Can I look at the horoscope of his wife? There may be some stars there to ensure long life for the husband".

Komalata-ammal immediately from her memory gave the details of Janaki's horoscope. With additional study, Narayanswamy added, "Yes, the bad effect of short life will be mitigated if his wife Janaki lives apart from Ramanujan".

Komalata-ammal with a deep sigh murmured, "I have been pleading him to send his wife to her father's home, but he utterly refuses. He will never agree to that".

10.4 The end came:

Ramanujan's doctors and friends were of the opinion that he had given up the will to live. Up to four days before death, he had been working on mathematics though. The health had taken tum for the worst. Doctors had said barring some miracle, no medicine can do any good and be trusted.

On 26th April, 1920, early in the morning he fainted, became unconscious. His wife sat down on his bed, feeding him sips of warm milk for about two hours. Beside wife Janaki, there were his father (Srinivasa Iyengar, who had lost sight), mother (Komalata-ammal), his two brothers (Lakshmi Narasimhan, and Thirunarayanan) and some friends. Parents of Janaki and her brother had arrived there two days before and were by his bedside. He died at mid-morning.

On that very day, 26th April in the afternoon, Ramachandra Rao, with the help of his son in-law C.S. Ramarao and Ramanujan's childhood friend Rajagopalachari, Ramanujan was cremated on the cremation ground near Chetput. His younger brother Lakshmi Narasimhanan was the person to complete the formal cremation ceremonial part. Thus, came the end of a great soul, Srinivasa Ramanujan. He was 32 years old.

It may be mentioned that as per tradition in India, in a funeral and after 13 days when the mourning period religiously ends, close friends and relatives along with some priests assemble at the family of the deceased and all dine together. However, the orthodox persons do not partake in it unless a social im-purification committed has not been ceremonially washed out, by prescribed atonement, the *paschatap.* It may be recalled that after returning from England, Ramanujan's mother wanted to take him to Rameshwaram for purification of the demerit of foreign travel. This had to be deferred at that time because of Ramanujan's ill health. Orthodox Brahmins in those days, and traditionally even now, are very particular in observing any social violations. For this reason in Ramanujan's death none of his relatives or priests came to attend his cremation or in the 13th day ceremony, when the mourning religiously ended.

□

11

Mourning & Remembering

News of Ramanujan's death appeared in all newspapers of Madras (now Chennai) and also in India nationwide. His death was mourned at several places in India, UK and other places through condolence meetings. His life sketch almost everywhere presented him as a super genius, a person in a short life of 32 years without education beyond school, in a poor family having worked as a clerk in Madras Port Trust, on research scholarship traveling to England, earning a B.A. and F.R.S., Fellowship of Trinity, and Professorship at Madras University.

His personal traits—orthodox Brahmanic values, spirituality, divine inspiration of Goddess Namagiri also drew quite some attention.

11.1 Obituary by Hardy in 'Nature':

Hardy was shocked to learn of Ramanujan's death. He wrote an obituary, which appeared in 1920 in the internationally top ranking magazine, '*Nature*'. Hardy observed that Ramanujan's work primarily involved fields less known even to the pure mathematicians.

He concluded his obituary with

> *"His insight into formulae was quite amazing, and altogether beyond anything I have met with in any European mathematician. It is perhaps useless to speculate as to his history had he been introduced to modern ideas and methods at sixteen instead of at twenty-six. It is not*

extravagant to suppose that he might have become the greater mathematician of his time. What he really did is wonderful enough, when the researches which his work has suggested have been completed, it will probably seem a good deal more wonderful than it does today".

Hardy further said:

"He combined a power of generalization, a feeling for form, and a capacity for rapid modification of his hypotheses that were often startling, and made him, in his peculiar field, without a rival in his day. The limitations of his knowledge were as startling as its profundity. Here was a man who could work out modular equations and theorems to orders unheard of, whose mastery of continued fractions was beyond that of any mathematician in the world, who had found for himself the functional equation of the zeta function and the dominant terms of the many of the most famous problems in the analytic theory of numbers, and yet he had never heard of a doubly periodic function or of Cauchy's theorem, and had indeed but the vaguest idea of what a function of complex variable was". (See, Wikipedia, the free encyclopedia).

When asked about the methods Ramanujan employed to arrive at this solutions, Hardy said that they were "arrived at by a process of mingled argument, intuition, and induction, of which he was entirely unable to give any coherent account". He also stated that he had "never met his equal, and can compare him only with Euler or Jacobi". (See, Wikipedia, the free encyclopedia).

11.2 Other important tributes:

Neville, who was instrumental in bringing Ramanujan from India to England, wrote an obituary that appeared in '*Proceedings of the London Mathematical Society*'. In fact later in 1941 he gave a talk on Ramanujan that was aired on radio. Part of his written article for the talk carried the following:

"Ramanujan's career, just because he was a mathematician, is of unique importance in the development of relations between India and England. India has produced great scientists, but Bose and Raman were educated outside India, and so one can say how much of their inspiration was derived from the great laboratories in which their formative years were spent and from the famous men who taught them...... Only in mathematics are the standards unassailable, and therefore of all Indians, Ramanujan was the first whom the English knew to be innately the equal of their greatest men. The mortal blow to the assumption, so prevalent in the western world, that white is intrinsically superior to black, the offensive assumption that has survived countless humanitarian arguments and political appeals and poisoned countless approaches to collaboration between England and India, was struck by the hand of Srinivasa Ramanujan".

In India, Ramanujan made every Indian proud of his rich heritage in mathematics—discovering a perfect number system, trigonometry, astronomy, in wide areas of algebra, etc. The lineage of great Aryabhata passed their minds.

The year after his death, *Nature* listed Ramanujan among other distinguished scientists and mathematicians on a "Calendar of Scientific Pioneers", who had achieved eminence. (See, Wikipedia, the free encyclopedia 73).

Journal of Indian Mathematical Society carried tributes to Ramanujan and said, *"He has raised India in the estimation of outside world".*

K. Srinivasa Rao has said, *"As for his place in the world of Mathematics, we quote Bruce* C. *Berndt:*

"Paul Erdös has passed on to us Hardy's personal ratings of mathematicians. Suppose that we rate mathematicians on the basis of pure talent on a scale 0 to 100, Hardy gave himself a score of 25, J.E. Littlewood 30, David Hilbert 80 and Ramanujan 100".

During a lecture at the Indian Institute of Technology (IIT) Madras, Chennai in May 2011, Berndt stated that over the last 40 years, as nearly all of Ramanujan's theorems have been proven right, there had been greater appreciation of Ramanujan's work and brilliance, and that Ramanujan's work was now pervading many areas of mathematics and physics. (See Wikipedia, the free encyclopedia).

11.3 Strong Indian nationalistic tributes:

Ramachandra Rao under strong Indian nationalistic fervor wrote:

"He [Ramanujan] whose name shed a luster on all India, whose career is understood as the severest condemnation of the present exotic system of education; whose name was always appealed to, if any one forgetful of India's past ventured to doubt her intellectual capabilities. Even when two Continents were publishing his results, he remained the same childish man, with style in dress or affectation of manner, with the same kind face, with same simplicity. Pilgrims came to Ramanujan's chambers and wondered if this was he.... If I am to sum up Ramanujan in one word, I would say, Indianality".

In a meeting of the *London Mathematical Society* held on June 10, 1920, the following was recorded,

"The President referred to the loss that the Society has suffered in the death of Mr. S. Ramanujan, and Major MacMahon spoke on the subject of Mr. Ramanujan's mathematical work".

In his book *Scientific Edge,* celebrated physicist Jayant Narlikar wrote:

"Srinivasa Ramanujan, was discovered by Cambridge mathematician Hardy, whose great mathematical findings were beginning to be appreciated from 1915 to

1919. His achievements were to be fully understood much later, well after his untimely death in 1920. For example, his work on the highly composite numbers (numbers with a large number of factors) started a whole new line of investigations in the theory of such numbers".

11.4 Ramanujan's family after his death:

Two days before the death of Ramanujan, his wife Janaki's parents and brother had arrived at Chetput, Madras. The family was under great stress, everybody grieving. Also, there existed lack of understanding, in fact hostility, between twenty year old Janaki and elderly mother of Ramanujan.

It was not possible for Janaki to stay there after the death of Ramanujan. So, after the death of Ramanujan, Janaki, with her mother, went to Rajendram, where her parents lived. Later she went to Bombay and started living with her brother's family there. It may be noted that amongst Hindus in general, and strictly in Brahmins, widows do not agree to remarriage.

After Ramanujan's death, the family of which an account follows below, 18 year old younger brother Lakshmi Narasimhan (who also later died at a young age), was the only person capable of writing, forwarding and contacting persons. He, to the best of his capability, started doing it and keeping date wise record of things in the name of Ramanujan's life and activities. Initially he also wrote to close family friends of the problems that family was facing.

Just three days after the death, on 29th April 1920, two letters were written to Hardy. The first from the Manager in Charge, of the Office of Registrar of the University of Madras said, "By direction of the Syndicate, I write to communicate to you, with feelings of deep regret, the sad news of the death of Mr. S. Ramanujan, F.R.S., which took place on the morning of the 26th April".

The other letter written by Lakshmi Narasimhan was as follows:

Dear Sir,

I am extremely very sorry to tell you that my brother Mr. S. Ramanujan F.R.S. died on 26th April at an early age of 32.

All his manuscripts that were in his trunk were handed over on the day of his death to Mr. Ramachandra Row's son-in-law, since the former is at Nilgris. Not only those but also the journals, magazines—all he possessed except the books he had, were taken away by them.....

All the books and all the suits and all things are entirely under the control of his wife. Mr. Ramachandra Row's son-in-law told me that.... He would make arrangements with Madras Government to send monthly installment of Rs. 50.00 or nearly £3/- to his wife. I am very sorry that why such an arrangement was not made for my family.

Sir, I have a lame grandmother who was greatly responsible for bringing my brother up and educating him. As soon as my brother's departure to England, my father has lost his two eyes and thus remained a blind man. ...His age is 65. Beside these, I have got a corpulent mother who resembles my brother in all physical features.

I have a younger brother reading in high school. I have no sisters. Coming to myself, I am a young man of 18 appeared this year for Intermediate Examination and while (my brother) was living here, I did not care for being wrapped myself in ecstasy I remained with him for the past one year and served him cordially.

I have no uncles or cousins to protect me. We have no property. I have a great desire to study. I have no taste, sorry to say, for mathematics. I like to read Shakespeare, Wordsworth I do not know how to feed them.

Therefore, I humbly request you to write to the Madras University to give a monthly allowance to us. I was told that my brother is entitled to get a sum from the Cambridge University.

.... Each single day passes with great difficulty. Unless

years of age. The widow is getting an annuity of Rs. 20/- or nearly 26s. per mensem from the Registrar and University of Madras for transferring rights to Ramanujan's mss. to the university. My own sons were getting Govt. scholarships with the concession that they were not required to pay fees.

Now, I have written to the Govt. of India to select my younger son S. Thirunarayanan, B.A. for the post of a probationary superintendent of post offices in India. The post of probationary superintendent carries a salary of £12/- per mensem and that of an inspector £6/- per mensem. I have also requested them to select my elder son S. Lakshmi Narasimhan for the post of an inspector of post offices in Madras. I have also mentioned in the application the various benefits conferred the bereaved members.

I have also requested Mr. Littlehailes M.A. (who was in 1914 Director of Public Instructions and who is now educational Commissioner with the Govt. of India) to recommend my two sons, the unfortunate brothers of the first Indian Fellow of the Royal Society, to the Govt. of India".

At the end of the letter, she gave her address and also same address for her son, Lakshmi Narasimhan.

Both the brothers, it was noted, obtained positions in Madras Post Office.

Brother Thirunarayanan continued to work in the Post office. The other brother Lakshmi Narasimhan passed away a few years later.

Wife Janaki-ammal lived a long life. She adopted a boy, Narayanan as her son who spent time with her and well cared for her. On 13th August, 1987 she was honored by the Institute of Mathematical Sciences, Chennai and the Hinduja Foundation.

Mrs. Janaki-Ammal with adopted son Narayanan, and his wife Vaidehi

Brother Thirunarayanan

□

12

Glimpses of Ramanujan's Mathematics

Ramanujan mathematical contributions are in several areas of mathematics and were made at different stages of his life. These are quite extensive as well. The way his mind worked has been more a mystery having admittedly transcendence input of his family Goddess. He was one of his own type of incredible mathematician generally one with unusual gift of imagination of the world of mathematics—a mathematician never seen before.

Professor Bruce Berndt,
Holding the slate Ramanujan worked his mathematics on

Professor Bruce Berndt of Illinois has worked on the three Notebooks for over 20 years. He has provided, in five Ramanujan's volumes, formal proofs of all the 3,542 results.

On time scale his contribution to mathematics can perhaps be divided into heads.

- Work in India before going to Cambridge.
- Work during time spent in Cambridge.
- Work done after returning to India before death.
- Work done in Cambridge, discovered about 55 years of his death.
- Work perhaps still lying somewhere unnoticed.

12.1 Work done in India before going to Cambridge:

This is the period from 1903 to 1914, and the results obtained by him during this period are in three parts and are all available in his three Notebooks. First Notebook has 16 chapters running in 134 pages. Second Notebook has 21 chapters running in 254 pages. The third Notebook has 33 pages. In these Notebooks, there are over 4000 results entered by Ramanujan, without proofs or hints. Some results in second Notebook are repeated from the first Notebook. If repeated results are counted once, then in all there are 3,542 theorems therein.

Of the work done in this first phase, his five papers were published in *'Journal of Indian Mathematical Society'* and five appeared in the same journal after reaching Cambridge.

12.2 Work done during five years of his stay in England:

Ramanujan carried with him his three Notebooks to Cambridge. He gave these to Prof Hardy and others to study. But according to a letter written to a friend, the way he was, while with Hardy, he did not get time to spend upon on his Notebooks material. Other new ideas took all his attention for researches there. Work done there appeared in papers published by Ramanujan there or in articles of Hardy, Littlewood, Watson etc. in different articles after his death.

A list of his twenty research papers and seven others jointly with Hardy can be found in Sections 14.4 and 14.5 of this book. His thirty seven research papers are available in the book *'Collected Papers by Srinivasa'* which has been edited by G.H, Hardy, P.V. Seshu Aiyar and B.M. Wilson (see Hardy, Seshu Aiyar and Wilson [8] in Section 14.2 of this book). In 1927, it was published by Cambridge University Press and later in 1962 by Chelsea.

Professor Hardy, who did the highly valuable work of providing support to Ramanujan, later in 1936 gave discourses on the work of Ramanujan. A collection of Hardy's 12 lectures appeared in the book *'Ramanujan: Twelve lectures on subjects suggested by his life and work'*, that was published by Cambridge University Press in 1940 (see Hardy [6] in Section 14.2 of this book). Titles of these 12 lectures are:

1. The Indian Mathematician Ramanujan
2. Ramanujan and the theory of prime numbers
3. Round numbers
4. Some more problems of the analytic theory of numbers
5. A lattice-point problem
6. Ramanujan's work on partitions
7. Hypergeometric series
8. Asymptotic theory of partitions
9. The representation of numbers as sum of squares
10. Ramanujan's function $\tau(n)$
11. Definite integrals
12. Elliptic and modular functions.

12.3 Work done after returning from England:

After returning to India, he continued to dedicatedly work on mathematics. He still used a slate for working details and expressions.

A major break-through received during this period was the definition of a totally novel, Mock-Theta functions. From India he wrote to Professor Hardy on it with some details.

12.4 Lost Notebook of Ramanujan—Work discovered in 1976:

There is an interesting story about it. Unexpectedly, in 1976 some unknown work of Ramanujan came to light. Its credit goes to Professor George E. Andrews. He called it, '*Lost Notebook of Ramanujan*'.

In April 1976, Professor George E. Andrews was to go for a one week long conference from Wisconsin to France. His wife and two daughters were to accompany him. As it happens, the airline fares were much cheaper if instead one week, the trip could be of three weeks. This needed something to keep Andrews and his three family members occupied for the extra time. Professor G.N. Watson, who had worked on Ramanujan's papers at Cambridge had died in 1965. A colleague suggested to Andrews that he could think of going to Cambridge and use his time there to go through the papers left behind by G.N. Watson. So a side trip to Cambridge was undertaken.

Watson, who was a FRS, when he died, Professor J.M. Whittaker, son of one of the collaborators of Watson was asked to write his obituary. In this process, a matter of 140 pages, in the hand writing of Ramanujan, was found. This had reached unattended at Trinity College. Andrews found in these pages, some of the matter on Mock-Theta functions, the subject of his own Ph.D. thesis. Andrews got thrilled, and with tireless efforts, he got a copy of the same. It bears signatures of Ramanujan on some pages; comments by Hardy on some pages, in their hand writings. Andrews settled that this matter is the work of Ramanujan. It was nearly 55 years after this treasure left by Ramanujan was discovered.

In 1984, Narosa Publishing House, republished '*Notebooks of Srinavasa Ramanujan*' that were earlier published in 1957 by Tata Institute of Fundamental Research, Bombay. And in 1987, the year of Ramanujan's birth centenary, with Introduction by George Andrews, a book appeared under the title, '*Srinivasa Ramanujan: The Lost Notebook And Other Unpublished Papers*'. In 9"x12" size it has 419 pages, with list of the contents as given below:

12.5 Possibly some work that may appear in future:

At the centenary celebration of Ramanujan, his wife, Janaki was interviewed. According to Bruce Berndt, Ramanujun's wife told him that while Ramanujan's cremation was going on, a teacher of Ramanujan came home and walked away with some of Ramanujan's papers. From this, it is inferred that some of the work done by Ramanujan in his last few days did not really reach Madras University.

Some results from his work:

Let us begin with his work on numbers and go briefly to other areas. His contemporaries and all his auto-biographers have uniformly stated that Ramanujan mastered personal close friendship with numbers. In Sanskrit there is term called *aashu'*- an *'aashu person'* means one who can answer/solve any question/ problem of any type right and instantly, even before, it is fully posed to him/her. Ramanujan was an *'aashu-mathematician'*. An illustration of the same is found in the following famous problem.

12.6 The Taxicab Number Problem:

When Ramanujan was ill and admitted in a hospital in Putney, Hardy came to see him by a taxi. With a view to start talking of numbers to lift the ailing mathematician's spirit, Hardy said, "I came here in a taxi with a very dull number 1729". But Ramanujan an aashu-friend of numbers jumped of the bed and cried, "No, Mr. Hardy—it is a very interesting number. It is the smallest number expressible as the sum of two distinct cubes!" ($1729 = 1^3 + 12^3 = 9^3 + 10^3$).

The matter did not end there. Hardy continued to find the smallest number which can be expressed as sum of fourth power in two different ways. Ramanujan's answer was, this should be a pretty big number. In fact that number is 635318657, found by Euler, with

$$635318657=158^4+59^4=133^4+134^4$$

This 'Taxicab problem'created quite some interest amongst mathematician. Silverman used it for explaining the 'elliptic curves'.

This instant observation by Ramanujan generated interest in finding other possible taxicab numbers. Their total number is six only. Also $1729 = 1^3 + 12^3 = 9^3 + 10^3$, can be seen as,

$$9^3+10^3=12^3+1, \text{ or } x^3+y^3= z^3+1,$$

a number, near in Fermat's theorem for n=3.

his own had independently derived this result, which was very creditable of him.

12.10 Nested square roots:

There are several rather simple but interesting results never seen before Ramanujan, in which nested square roots occur. Below, we state and prove the following two:

(a) $3=\sqrt{1+2\sqrt{1+3\sqrt{1+4\sqrt{.....}}}}$

(b) $4=\sqrt{6+2\sqrt{7+3\sqrt{8+4\sqrt{.....}}}}$

Solution: We have

$$n(n+2)=n\sqrt{(n+2)^2}=n\sqrt{n^2+4n+4)}==n\sqrt{1+(n+1)((n+3)}.$$

Now let f (n)=n(n+2). Then

$$f(n)=n\sqrt{1+f(n+1)}=n\sqrt{1+(n+1)\sqrt{1+f(n+2)}}$$

$$n(n+2)=n\sqrt{1+(n+1)\sqrt{1+(n+2)\sqrt{1+(n+3)}.....}}$$

Next putting n=1, we get the result (a).

To prove result (b), we have

$$n(n+3)=n\sqrt{n^2+6n+9}=n\sqrt{(n+5)+(n+1)(n+4)}$$

Taking $f(n)=n(n+3)=n\sqrt{(n+5)+f(n+1)}$

$$=n\sqrt{(n+5)+(n+1)\sqrt{(n+6)+f(n+2)}}$$

gives

$$n(n+3)=n\sqrt{(n+5)+(n+1)\sqrt{(n+6)+(n+2)\sqrt{(n+7)+...}}}$$

Now, putting n=1, in above, we get (b).

12.11 Highly Composite Numbers:

During second year in England, Ramanujan produced many more new and original papers, out of which some were with Hardy while some were all of his own. In this period, Ramanujan worked on the distribution of prime numbers, the Riemann hypothesis, prime factorization of integers and more. In 1915, Ramanujan introduced a new concept of the *highly composite numbers.*

We well know of prime numbers and composite numbers. According to the Fundamental Theorem of Arithmetic, every number can be uniquely represented as product of powers of prime numbers. A composite numbers has divisors more than 1 and itself, For example $360 = 2^3.3^2.5$ is a composite number, with 24 divisors, namely 1, 2, 4, 8, 3, 6, 12, 24, 9, 18, 36, 72, 5, 10, 20, 40, 15, 45, 30, 60, 120, 10, 180, and 360.

Ramanujan defined *n* as a highly composite number if the number of divisors *of n* is more than that of any its predecessors. Thus 6 is a highly composite number, because it has four divisors 1, 2, 3 and 6 while its predecessors namely 1,2,3,4,5 (less than 6) have less than 4 divisors. On the other hand number 2,000 is not highly composite, as its divisors are 20, but a predecessor 360 less than it has 24 divisors.

It may be noted that if a number $= 2^a.3^b.5^c.....p^l$, then its total number of different divisors are,

$$(a+1)(b+1)(c+1)...(l+1).$$

Ramanujan proved following two results on highly composite numbers:

<u>First Result:</u> If $N= 2^a.\ 3^b.\ 5^c.....p^l$ is a highly composite number then $a \geq b \geq c \geq ... \geq l \geq 1$; and if N is very big, then $a > b > c > ... > l > 1$, with strict inequalities at every place.

<u>Second Result:</u> The powers of primes involved in increasing order form a regularly decreasing chain followed by all 1's.

For example $N = 674632858800 = 2^6\ 3^4\ 5^2\ 7^2.\ 11.13.17.19.23$

Ramanujan noted 100 numbers of this type in his 'Notebook'. He was perhaps visualizing some pattern or some more revealing results of these numbers.

12.12 Partitions of Integers:

In this area, Ramanujan worked in collaboration with Hardy and proved some very elegant results including congruence properties. A partition of an integer *n* is a division of *n* into number of positive integral parts. The number of partitions of *n* is denoted by p(n). For example:

$n = 3$, partitions of 3 are: 3, 2+1, 1+1+1, $p(3) = 3$

$n = 4$, partitions of 4 are: 4, 3+1, 2+2, 2+ 1+1, 1+1+1+1, $p(4) = 5$

$n = 5$, partitions of 5 are: 5, 4+1, 3+2, 3 + 1+1, 2 +2+1, 2+1+1+1, 1+1+1+1+1, $p(5) = 7$, etc.

Readers can verify that, $p(20)=629$, $p(24)=1575$, $p(49)=173525$, $p(100) = 190569292$.

Every number has definite number of partitions and they increase quite fast. It may be mentioned here that Euler (1707–1783) had started work on partitions. After Euler, in over 150 years, many formulas and recurrence relations on them have appeared. Algebra was basically used in deriving these. Ramanujan and Hardy are the first to use complex analysis in obtaining some significant results on partitions.

Ramanujan proved that if *n* is of the type $5m–1$, $7m–2$, *or* $11m– 6$, then *p(n)* is respectively divisible by 5, 7 and 11.

Numbers 4, 9, 14, 19 of the form $5m- 1$, with p(4) = 5, p(9) = 30, p(14) = 135, p(19) =490 are all divisible by 5. In this direction Ramanujan proved many surprising results.

On partitions, Ramanujan's work continued after returning to India from Cambridge. In the book *Hardy & Wright, 'An Introduction to the Theory of Numbers'*, identities obtained by Ramanujan given are as follows:

$$p(5m + 4) = 0 \ (mod\ 5)$$

$$p(7m + 5) = 0 \ (mod\ 7)$$

$$p(11\,m + 6) = 0 \ (mod\ 11)$$

Ramanujan also proved following congruencies with moduli $5^2, 7^2, 11^2$.

$$p(25m + 24) = 0 \ (mod\ 5^2)$$

$$p(49m + 47) = 0 \ (mod\ 7^2)$$

$$p(121m + 116) = 0 \ (mod\ 11^2)$$

He went ahead for good deal of further results conjecturing if $\delta = 5^a\, 7^b\, 11^c$ and $24\lambda \equiv 1 \pmod{\delta}$, then $p(m\,\delta + \lambda) \equiv 0 \pmod{\delta}$.

Though there were counter examples to this conjecture in some cases, its following case was later proved by Krccmar: $p(125m + 99) = 0 \ (mod\ 5^3)$.

Ramanujan established following, according to Hardy, most outstanding identity:

$$p(4)+p(9)\,y+p(14)\,y^2+.....=\frac{5[(1-y^5)(1-y^{10})(1-y^{15})...]^5}{[(1-y)(1-y^2)(1-y^3)...]^6}$$

12.13 Some approximations of π:

The year Ramanujan arrived in England, he published his first paper in "The Quarterly Journal of Mathematics", a well-known British journal. The paper was titled *'Modular Equations and Approximations to Pi'*. It included a large number of amazing formulas for approximations of π, well-known as the ratio of the circumference of a circle to its diameter.

The number π is an example of an *irrational number*, a number that cannot be expressed as the simple ratio of two integers, implying that its decimal expansion is infinite, running forever without a discernible pattern, in contrast to the pattern seen in the decimal expansion of the number

$$\frac{3}{7} = 0.428571428571.....,$$

which is a *rational number*. Although π can be easily described as a simple ratio of the circumference of a circle to its diameter, it is not simple or easy to calculate its decimal places. Below, we give some of the formulas that Ramanujan obtained in the above mentioned paper published in Quarterly Journal of Mathematics.

1. $\pi = \frac{19}{16}\sqrt{7} = 3.14180\ldots$

2. $\pi = \frac{63}{25}\left(\frac{17+15\sqrt{5}}{7+15\sqrt{5}}\right) = 3.1415926358....$

3. $\pi = \left(9^2 + \frac{19^2}{22}\right)^{1/4} = 3.141592642....$

4. $\pi = \frac{12}{\sqrt{130}} log\left[\frac{\left(2+\sqrt{5}\right)(3+\sqrt{13}}{\sqrt{2}}\right]$ correct up to 15 places

5. $\pi = \frac{4}{\sqrt{522}} Ð \left[\frac{\left(Ð+\sqrt{\ }\right)}{\sqrt{2}}\left(5\sqrt{29}+11\sqrt{6}\right)\right]\left[\left(\frac{9+3\sqrt{6}}{4}\right)^{1/2} + \left(\frac{5+3\sqrt{6}}{4}\right)^{1/2}\right],$
correct up to 31 places

6. $\frac{4}{\pi} = 1 + \frac{7}{4}\left(\frac{1}{2}\right)^{Ð} + \frac{13}{4^2}\left(\frac{1.3}{2.4}\right) + \frac{19}{4^3}\left(\frac{1.3.5}{2.4.6}\right) + \ldots$

7. $\frac{32}{\pi} = \left(5\sqrt{5}-1\right) + \frac{47\sqrt{5}+29}{64}\left(\frac{1}{2}\right)^3\left(\frac{\sqrt{5}-1}{2}\right)^8 + \frac{89\sqrt{5}+59}{64^2}\left(\frac{1.3}{2.4}\right)^3\left(\frac{\sqrt{5}-1}{2}\right)^{16} + ...$
Here it may be noted that $\left(5\sqrt{5}\ \ 1\right), 47\sqrt{5}\ \ 29, 89\sqrt{5}\ \ 59, ...$ form arithmetic progression, with common difference $42\sqrt{5}+30$.

8. $\frac{1}{\pi} = \frac{2\sqrt{2}}{9801}\sum_{0}^{\infty}\frac{(4k)!}{(k!)^4\,4^{4k}}\frac{(1103+26390k)}{99^{4k}}$

It may be remarked that after ninety-nine years of Ramanujan's paper with G.H. Hardy, while working in England, which was published in the Quarterly Journal of Mathematics, XLV (1914), 350-372, the Russian-American brothers David and Gregory Chudnovsky by using a home-built supercomputer ran a variant of Ramanujan's formula

$$\frac{1}{\pi}=\frac{2\sqrt{2}}{9801}\sum_{0}^{\infty}\frac{(4k)!}{(k!)^{4}\,4^{4k}}\frac{(1103+26390k)}{99^{4k}},$$

to determine the first 12.1 trillion digits of this number (with earlier estimates of ten trillion digits of π in 2011 and five million digits in 2010). Their algorithm uses a very simple converging infinite series, related to the above Ramanujan's original formula. This work opens the way to very similar, yet more and more accurate, ways of obtaining more and more digits of π.

12.14 Some Integrals:

Ramanujan had special expertise on definite integrals. He worked on them at an earlier stage of his research career in India and these appeared in his several research publications.

There is a full chapter on definite integrals in Hardy's book (see [6] in Section 14.2 of this book), *Ramanujan: Twelve Lectures on Subjects Suggested by His Life and Work.* In this chapter, Professor Hardy has included only those that Ramanujan discovered before going to England and which Professor Watson also picked up. The two that he specially selected are:

$$\int_{0}^{\infty}x^{s-1}\left[\varnothing(0)-x\varnothing(1)+x^{2}\varnothing(2)-\ldots\right]dx=\frac{\pi}{sinx\pi}\varnothing(-s)$$

and,

$$\int_{0}^{\infty}x^{s-1}\left[\lambda(0)\frac{x}{1!}\lambda(1)+\frac{x^{2}}{2!}\lambda(2)-\ldots\right]dx=\Gamma(s)\lambda(-s).$$

In his '*Lost Book*'there are about 50 definite integrals. Several of these are on Mordell Integrals.

His definite integrals are not simple. For example, look at the following:

$$\int_0^\infty \frac{1+\left(\frac{x}{b+1}\right)^2}{1+\left(\frac{x}{a}\right)^2} \cdot \frac{1+\left(\frac{x}{b+2}\right)^2}{1+\left(\frac{x}{a+1}\right)^2} \ldots dx = \frac{\pi^{1/2}}{2} \frac{\Gamma\left(a+\frac{1}{2}\right)\Gamma(b+1)\Gamma\left(b-a+\frac{1}{2}\right)}{\Gamma(a)\Gamma\left(b+\frac{1}{2}\right)\Gamma(b-a+1)},$$

and

$$\int_0^\infty \frac{dx}{\left(1+x^2\right)\left(1+r^2x^2\right)\left(1+r^4x^2\right)\ldots.} = \frac{\pi}{2\left(1+r+r^3+r^6+r^{10}+\ldots\right)}.$$

12.15 Continued fractions:

Ramanujan was very comfortable in expressing various expressions and integrals as continued fractions and to use them for solving many combinatorial problems. Below we give two continued fractions equivalent to two definite integrals.

a. $$\int_0^a \text{Đ}^{-x^2} = \frac{\pi^{\text{Đ}}}{2} - \cfrac{e^{-a^2}}{2a+\cfrac{1}{a+\cfrac{2}{2a+\cfrac{3}{a+\cfrac{4}{2a+\ldots}}}}}$$

b. $$\int_0^\infty \frac{xe^{-x\sqrt{5}}\,dx}{\cosh x} = \cfrac{1}{1+\cfrac{1^2}{1+\cfrac{1^2}{1+\cfrac{2^2}{1+\cfrac{2^2}{1+\cfrac{3^2}{1+\cfrac{3^2}{1+\ldots}}}}}}}$$

12.16 Ramanujan's Tau Function:

In 1916, Ramanujan defined tau (τ), a function obtained by multiplying infinitely many polynomials together. He obtained,

$$\tau(1) = 1, \tau(2) = -24, \tau(3) = 252, \tau(4) = -1472,$$

$$\tau(5) = 4830, \tau(6) = -6048, \tau(7) = -16744, \ldots.,$$

and values of tau function for values up to n = 816212624008487344127999, have been calculated by mathematicians.

Ramanujan observed, without proof, the following three properties of tau functions:

$\tau(mn) = \tau(m)\tau(n)$, if $gcd(m,n) = 1$

$\tau(p^{r+1}) = \tau(p)\,\tau(p^r) - p^{11}\,\tau(p^{r-1})$ for p prime and $r > 0$.

$|\tau(p)| \leq 2p^{11/2}$, for all prime p.

The tau function satisfies several congruence relations.

12.17 The Ramanujan Conjecture:

The Ramanujan conjecture is an assertion on the size of the tau-function, which has as generating function the discriminant modular form. It was finally proved as a consequence of Pierre Deligne's proof of the André Wei1 conjectures. Pierre Deligne won Fields Medal for his work in 1973. Ramanujan proved many congruence for these numbers, such as $\tau(p) \equiv 1+p^{11}$ mod 691for primes p. This congruence and others like it that Ramanujan proved inspired Jean-Pierre Serre, who won Fields Medal in 1954, to conjecture that there is a theory of Galois representations which explains these congruencies and more generally all modular forms. Serre's this conjecture was proved by Pierre Deligne which won him the Fields Medal. It may be remarked that the proof of Fermat's Last Theorem proceeds by first interpreting the elliptic curve and modular forms in terms of these Galois representations. Thus, without this theory there would have been perhaps no proof of Fermat's Last Theorem.

12.18 The Ramanujan-Fourier Transform:

In the area of analogue signal processing, we often use mathematical technique called Fourier Transform. When w enter the digital world, a different tool called Discrete Fourie Transform is used. If one has to analyze noise signals, engineer have recently concluded that the more efficient mathematical too is perhaps the Ramanujan Fourier Transformation or briefly RF This shows that although Ramanujan worked on the Ramanuja Fourier Transform only to satisfy his urge to explore the beauty o mathematics, his work six decades later came out to be of use i day-to-day applications, like communications.

Some other problems of Ramanujan's master touch an vision are Magic Squares, Seventeen Mock-Theta Functions, an of course the famous 'Squaring a Circle'.

13

Legacy of Ramanujan, Today

As much as we explore, Ramanujan stands before us as a phenomenon—a mystery unresolved through his mathematics and more about his life events. Reflecting on his contributions and life, there obviously arise more questions. When his American biographer Robert Kanigel called him *'The Man Who Knew Infinity'*, one still feels short of the proper words to describe him.

Reflecting on Ramanujan's own words *"An equation for me has no meaning unless it expresses a thought of God"*, one feels that he was in fact in communication with God, which he unhesitatingly named Goddess Namagiri. Thus, perhaps, one can say for him *"The Man Who Knew God"*.

This reminds us of a deep Upanishadic Sanskrit aphorism *'Satyam Gyan Anantam Brahma'*.In this aphorism *'Brahma'*, from which the word Brahmin is derived, stands for all powerful Absolute Reality embodiment of all Existence, total Knowledge and Infinity.

Ramanujan occupies a unique place among the all-time great mathematicians of the world. The greatest legacy is his inspiring life and the way he received support from persons initially in India including British officials, from Madras University, crossing all boundaries for promoting creativity and excellence, later 'God Sent' support of G.H. Hardy and other academicians.

He should not be a forgotten person, not just known a prodigy. Not only India, the world has greatly supported and felt proud of Ramanujan. There are lot of activities that have been organized at different levels to keep the legacy of Ramanujan alive. In this chapter, we have made an attempt to briefly mention some of these activities.

13.1 Ramanujan's Birthday, *the National Mathematics Day in India:*

Ramanujan's home state of Tamil Nadu in India celebrates 22nd December, the Ramanujan birthday, as 'State IT Day'.

A stamp picturing Ramanujan was released by the Government of India in 1962, at the 75-th anniversary of Ramanujan's birth to commence his achievements in the field of number theory.

Later, the Indian Postal Service issued a new design of this stamp on 22nd December 2011, the 125th anniversary of Ramanujan's birth.

Also, on 22nd December 2011, the 125th anniversary of Ramanujan's birth, the Government of India declared that this day will be celebrated every year as *National Mathematics Day.*

The then Prime Minister, Dr. Manmohan Singh also declared that the year 2012 would be celebrated as the *National Mathematics Year.* It may be noted that the year 2012 is important because it was in 1912 when Ramanujan got a temporary position in the Madras Accountant General's office on a salary of 20 Rupees per month, which lasted only a few weeks. However, toward the end of this assignment he applied and got position as a clerk under the Chief Accountant of the Madras Port Trust.

Since Ramanujan's centennial year, the Government Arts College, Kumbakonam where Ramanujan studied, celebrates 22nd December, Ramanujan's buthday, as Ramanujan Day.

The Indian Institute of Technology Madras (IIT, Madras) in Chennai also observes Ramanujan's birthday, 22nd December as Ramanujan Day.

13.2 Srinivasa Ramanujan Centre —SASTRA:

As has been mentioned in Chapter 1, in 1984 Shanmugba College of Engineering was established in Thanjavur (formerly known as Tanjore), of which Kumbakonam is a municipal town. In the year 2001, this college was renamed as Shanmugha Science, Technology& Research Academy (SASTRA).

On April 26, 2001, the Government of India conferred to SASTRA the status of a 'Deemed University'.This university now offers various undergraduate and post graduate courses in Engineering, Science, Education, Management, Law and Arts including many Doctoral programs. It has well-equipped laboratories, a well-stocked library and one of the best computing facilities in India. It is a private university, but since its establishment this has grown by leaps and bounds and attracts some of the brightest students and faculty kom India and abroad.

In 2003, SASTRA University opened a branch campus in Kumbakonam, which is known as *Srinivasa Ramanujan* — ***SASTRA*** *Center.* This center was dedicated to the Nation on December 20, 2003 by His Excellency Dr. A.P.J. Abdul Kalam, who was at that time, the President of India.

Activities of the Srinivasa Ramanujan Centre were expanded with SASTRA UNIVERSITY when it acquired 10 acres of land in Lakshmivilas Agraharam area and constructed a massive six storied structure encompassing an area of 1,52,523 sq. ft. Situated in the heart of the town where Ramanujan lived, this building houses class rooms, Computer laboratories, Electrical Machines laboratory, Electronics and Communications laboratory,

Physics laboratory, Chemistry and Biochemistry laboratory, Mechanical Workshops, a big auditorium, and a library to meet the requirements of students, faculty and staff members. Also, on this campus exists *The House of Ramanujan,* which SASTRA bought and converted it into a 'museum on life and work'of the Mathematical genious Srinivasa Ramanujan.

13.3 SASTRA Ramanujan Award:

To mark the occasion of the purchase of Ramanujan's Home, the SASTRA University organized an *'International Conference on Number Theory for Secure Communications,* at Kumbakonam campus from December 20 to December 22, 2003. The conference coincided with the 116th Birth Anniversary of Srinivasa Ramanujan, and was inaugurated by His Excellency Dr. A.P.J. Abdul Kalam, the then President of India. For more details about this award, we refer to the article, The SASTRA Ramanujan Prize: Its Origin and Its Winners by Krishnaswami Alladi (see [2] in Section 14.3 of this book) and attached as an Appendix to this book.

Professor Krishnaswami Alladi

The participants at the conference suggested that SASTRA should conduct such conferences every year around Ramanujan's birthday on different areas of Mathematics influenced by Ramanujan. This suggestion was accepted by the Dean of the

University and accordingly the Second SASTRA Ramanujan Conference was thus held in 2004 and inaugurated by Professor Krishnaswami Alladi, a well-known mathematician, Professor of Mathematics at the University of Florida, Gainesville, USA In this conference, Professor Alladi also delivered the concluding Ramanujan Commemoration Lecture.

Before Professor Alladi was to present his inaugural address, the then Vice-Chancellor of SASTRA Dr. Sethuraman told Professor Alladi that he will like to give $10,000.00 every year for a worthy cause in the name of Srinivasa Ramanujan, a generous offer which Dr. Alladi immediately accepted and suggested to consider creating a SASTRA-Ramanujan Prize, to be given annually to young mathematicians not exceeding the age of 32 years for outstanding contributions on theme related to number theory and allied areas, influenced by Srinivasa Ramanujan. The age limit for the prize was set at 32 because Ramanujan achieved so much in his brief life of 32 years.

The Vice-Chancellor immediately accepted the proposal and the creation of this award was announced by Dr. Alladi on December 20, 2004. The first SASTRA Ramanujan Prize was awarded in the SASTRA-Ramanujan Conference held in 2005 and since then it has continuously been awarded every year. This gives the brief description of how the SASTRA-Ramanujan Prize was instituted.

Given below are the awardees since 2005. It may be mentioned that four of the SASTRA- Ramanujan awardees have won **Fields Medal,** highest prize in Mathematics, awarded every four years.

The 2005 SASTRA Ramanujan Prize was awarded to **Manjul Bhargava** of the Princeton University, and **Kannan Soundararajan** of the University of Michigan. Both these mathematicians, Bhargava and Soundarajan were ranked as strong young mathematicians in the areas of algebraic number theory and analytic number theory respectively. Since both were ranked #1 by the Committee, the committee recommended that both be awarded two full prizes, and the award should not be split, to which the Vice-Chancellor of SASTRA University agreed. After receiving SASTRA Ramanujan prize in 2005, Professor Bhargava received AMS Cole Prize in 2008 and the Fields Medal in 2014. On the other hand, Soundararajan was subsequently recognized with Infosys Prize and the Ostrowski Prize, both in 2011.

The 2006 SASTRA Ramanujan Prize was awarded to **Terence Tao** of the University of California at Los Angeles (UCLA). Professor Tao was also recognized with the Fields Medal in 2006. He has made far-reaching contributions to several areas of Mathematics that include number theory, harmonic analysis, partial differential equations and ergodic theory. He is presently at the University of California, Los Angeles holding James and Carol Collins Chair of mathematics.

The 2007 SASTRA Ramanujan Prize was awarded to **Ben Green** from U.K. who solved the Cameron-Erdös conjecture. He is a Fellow of the Royal Society of London and is presently Waynf Herchel Smith Professor of Pure Mathematics at Oxford University, England.

The 2008 SASTRA Ramanujan Prize was awarded to **Akshay Venkatesh,** of Stanford University, USA. After the SASTRA Ramanujan Prize he was recognized with Infosys Prize in 2016, and the Ostrowski Prize in 2017. In 2018, he received the Fields Medal and is presently a faculty of the Institute of Advanced Study, Princeton.

The 2009 SASTRA Ramanujan Prize was awarded to **Kathrin Bringmann** of the University of Cologne, Germany and the University of Minnesota, USA for her work related to Ramanujan's Mock Theta functions, studied by Ramanujan in his *Lost Notebook,* the loose sheet of papers in which he wrote hundreds of formulas shortly before his death in 1920.

The 2010 SASTRA Ramanujan Prize was awarded **to Wei Zhang,** who has been doing outstanding work on relative trace formulas, and on Shimura varieties. When Zhang received the SASTRA Ramanujan Award in 2010 he was the Benjamin Pierce Instructor at the Department of Mathematics, Harvard University, USA, but now he is a full professor at Columbia University.

The 2011 SASTRA Ramanujan Prize was awarded to **Roman Holowinsky,** for his outstanding contributions at the interface of analytic number theory and the theory of modular forms. In collaboration with Kannan Soundararajan, he solved an important special case of well-known Quantum Unique Ergodicity Conjecture. At the time he received the award, he was an Assistant Professor at the Department of Mathematics, Ohio State University, Columbus, Ohio, USA.

The 2012 SASTRA Ramanujan Prize was awarded **to Zhiwei Yun,** who had just completed a C. L. E. Moore Instructorship at the Massachusetts Institute of Technology to take up a permanent faculty position at Stanford University in California. In 1918, Yuri received the prestigious New Horizons Prize in Mathematics.

The 2013 SASTRA Ramanujan Prize was awarded to **Peter Scholze** of the University of Bonn, Germany, for his revolutionary contributions to arithmetic algebraic geometry and the theory of automorphism forms. When Scholze received SASTRA Ramanujan Prize he was only 25 years of age, youngest to win this award. In 2015, he received the AMS Cole Prize, Fermat Prize and Leibniz Prize. In 2018, he was recognized with the Fields Medal, highest prize in Mathematics.

The 2014 SASTRA Ramanujan Prize was awarded **to James Maynard** of Oxford University, England, and the University of Montreal, Canada for his outstanding contributions to some of the most famous problems in Prime Numbers. He was also later recognized with Whitehead Prize in 2015 and the EMS Prize in 2016. Presently, he is a Professor at the Oxford University.

The 2015 SASTRA Ramanujan Prize was awarded to **Jacob Tsimerman** from the University of Toronto, Canada, for his outstanding contributions to diverse parts of Number Theory and in particular to André – Oort Conjecture, which he announced just before receiving the SASTRA Ramanujan Prize.

The 2016 SASTRA Ramanujan prize was shared by **Kaisa Matomaki of** the University of Turku, Finland and Maksym Radziwill of McGill University, Canada. Sarvadaman Chowla Conjecture is still unsolved but in 2016 Matomaki, Radziwill, and Terrence Tao proved a special case of this conjecture.

The 2017 SASTRA Ramanujan prize was awarded **to Maryna Viazovska** of the Swiss Federal Institute of Technology, Lausanne, Switzerland for her stunning solution in dimension 8 of the Sphere-Packing Problem.

The 2018 SASTRA Ramanujan prize was shared by **Yifeng Liu** of Yale University, USA and Jack Thorine of Cambridge University, England for their outstanding contributions to algebraic geometry, authomorphic representations, and number theory.

It may be remarked that since the beginning, the Ramanujan Prize Committee has always been chaired by Professor Krishnaswami Alladi of the University of Florida, Gainsville, USA.

13.4 The Ramanujan Journal:

The Ramanujan Journal, an international journal devoted to the areas of mathematics influenced by Ramanujan was started in 1997 and has since then been published regularly. Presently its Editor-in-Chief is Professor Krishnaswami Alladi and Managing Editor Professor Frank Garvan, both from University of Florida, Gainsville, USA. with editorial board consisting of some of the top mathematicians in the field, like Professors George Andrews from Pennsylvania State University, and Fields Medalist Manjul Bhargava from Princeton.

The remarkable discoveries made by Srinivasa Ramanujan have made a great impact on several branches of Mathematics, revealing deep and fundamental connections, and the Ramanujan Journal publishes papers of the highest quality in all areas of mathematics influenced by Ramanujan which includes: Hyper-geometric and basic hyper-geometric series (q-series), Partitions, Compositions and combinatory analysis, Circle method and asymptotic formulae.

13.5 Hardy-Ramanujan Journal:

This journal started in 1978 with R. Balasubramanian and K. Ramachandra as its founding editors. The first 33 volumes of this journal also carried a subheading 'A Journal devoted to primes, Diophantine equations, transcendental numbers and other questions on 1, 2, 3, 4, 5,..' and the original aims of this initiative were clearly expressed in the first volume. But, about two years after the passing away of K. Ramachandra in 2011, a decision to continue this journal was taken by a new team of editors, consisting mostly of people who took interest in and had contributed to the journal in the past, keeping the overall aim of the journal as when it was founded, and thus the combined Volumes 34 & 35 and Volume 36 were released in August and December of 2013 respectively, with just Hardy Ramanujan Journal as the title.

13.6 Some more activities recognizing Ramanujan:

Long ago, the International Center for Theoretical Physics (ICTP), Triste, Italy created in *Ramanujan's name,* a prize for young mathematicians from developing countries.

Vasavi College of Engineering, Hyderabad, India recognized as "The Best Engineering College of the state of Andhra Pradesh by the Indian Society of Technical Education" has named the building of its Department of Computer Science and Information Technology as '*Ramanujan Block*'.

In the book, *Hyperspace* by Michchio Kaku, Ramanujan's contributions to Superstring Theory and a brief synopsis of his life are given in *Part II* of this book.

On March 22, 1988, the PBS (Public Broadcasting Service) series *NOVA* aired a documentary on Ramanujan, *"The Man Who Loved Numbers"* (Season 15, Episode 19).

The novel *The Indian Clerk* by David Leavitt explores in fiction the events following Ramanujan's letter to G.H. Hardy.

In a recent production, *A Disappearing Number* by the company Complicite had explored the relationship between Hardy and Ramanujan.

In 2012, on the125th birthday of Ramanujan, Google honored him by replacing its logo with a doodle on its home page.

A play, *A First Class Man* by Alter Ego Productions, was based on David Freeman's *First Class Man.* The play is centered on Ramanujan and his complex and dysfunctional relationship with G.H. Hardy. On October 16, 2011, it was announced that Roger Spottiswoode, well known for his James Bond Film *Tomorrow Never Dies,* is working on the film version, starring actor Siddharth. Like the book and play, this film will also be titled *The First Class Man.*

In 2014, the film *Ramanujan,* an Indo-British collaboration film, which chronicles the life of Ramanujan, was released.

The book *The Man Who Knew infinity. A Life of the Genius Ramanujan* (ISBN number 978-0-684-19259-8) by Robert Kenigale was written and published in 1991 by Washington Square Press. The book gives a detailed account of Ramanujan's upbringing in India, his mathematical achievements, and his mathematical collaboration with his British Mathematics Advisor Professor G.H. Hardy.

13.7 A Pressman Film—*The Man Who Knew Infinity:*

As mentioned earlier, based on the above mentioned book, *The Man Who Knew Infinity* by Robert Kenigale, a Pressman film *The Man Who Knew Infinity* was released. In the film, Ramanujan is portrayed by British actor Dev Patel and G.H. Hardy by Hollywood actor Jeremy Irons. The film is directed by Matthew Brown and produced by Edward R. Pressman, Jim Young, Joe Thomas and Mark Montgomery (Executive Producers). The filming of this film began in August 2014 at Trinity College, Cambridge. It had its world premiere as a gala presentation on 17th September 2015 at the Toronto International Film Festival, and was selected as the opening gala for the 2015 Zurich Film Festival. It was also played at other film festivals including Singapore International Film Festival and Dubai International Film Festival. The film offers an in-depth view of one of the human stories behind the mathematical achievements that one takes for granted in everyday life. Mathematicians Ken Ono and Fields Medalist Manjul Bhargava collaborated in the production of the film by being advisors concerning mathematics, and are thus the Associate Producers of the film.

13.8 Ramanujan STEM Talent Initiative Awards:

In order to honor the legacy of Srinivasa Ramanujan, the Templeton World Charity Foundation, in conjunction with IFC Films and Pressman Film, producers of the motion picture *The Man Who Knew Infinity,* inspired by the life of Srinivasa Ramanujan created *The Spirit of Ramanujan* ***STEM*** *(Science, Technology, Engineering and Mathematics) Talent Initiative* to support emerging engineers, mathematicians, and scientists who lack traditional institutional support through financial grants and mentorship opportunities. The Spirit of Ramanujan Math STEM Talent Initiative strives to find undiscovered STEM talent around the world, for which it scans the globe for this talent. *The Spirit of Ramanujan* ***STEM*** *Talent Initiative Awards* are presented by Ken Ono, Asa Griggs Candler Professor of Mathematics at Emory University, USA, who recently moved to Virginia University, USA as Thomas Jefferson Professor of Mathematics.

Selected individuals, whose numbers can be in dozens, are awarded Templeton- Ramanujan Scholarly Development Prizes and/or Fellowships to use for furthering their educational pursuits and development. In the spirit of Ramanujan, fellowship recipients are offered financial support that can be spent on approved summer research/training in STEM subjects such as Awesome Math, Canada/USA Mathcamp, Modern Mathematics, PROMYS, Ross Mathematics, the REU in Arithmetic Geometry and Number Theory at Emory University, to name a few.

The list of inaugural winners include Bishoy Adel (Egypt), Kendall Clark (Maryland, USA), Dean Cureton (Georgia, USA), Sanath Devalapurkar (India), Martin Irungu (Kenya), Ishwar Karthik (Qatar), Catherine Yeo (California, USA) and Weitao Zhu (China).

The idea behind creating *The Spirit of Ramanujan* ***STEM*** *Talent Initiative Awards* is that greatness and talent can be found even in the most unexpected of circumstances, like Ramanujan was a two-time college dropout who hailed from a village in southern part of India, and what if Ramanujan had not written to Professor G.H. Hardy or what if Professor Hardy had not responded to his request to help. In fact, there are Ramanujans all over the world who need to be discovered and brought to light, like Ishwar Karthik, a 10 year old boy from Qatar who was awarded *the Inaugural Spirit of Ramanujan* ***STEM*** *Talent Initiative Award* has been working in complete isolation on Mathematics in Qatar, and he discovered at his own a method for computing digits of number π.

13.9 Centenary Celebrations of Ramanujan becoming F.R.S.:

As has been mentioned earlier, on 28th February 1918, Ramanujan, just 31 years old, became the youngest Fellow in the history of the Royal Society of London. As mentioned earlier, he was second Indian to have this honor, the first was Ardaseer Curseijee, a shipbuilder and engineer from India who was elected way back in 1841.

Prof. Ken Ono, Atlanta, USA

Prof. Manjul Bhargava, Princeton, USA

The year 2018 has been the centenary of Ramanujan's election as Fellow to the Royal Society of London, and to mark this event the Royal Society organized a gala event *"Srinivasa Rmanaujan, In celebration of the centenary of his election as F.R.S"*., during October 15-16, 2018 in London. In this event, the addresses were made by many mathematicians, including Professors George E. Andrews, Manjul Bhargava, Ken Ono and Robert C. Vaughan, F.R.S., who spoke on Ramanujan's mathematics and its extraordinary legacy across many fields.

13.10 Ramanujan Mathematical Society:

It is an organization of persons formed with the aim of 'promoting mathematics at all levels'. The Society was founded in 1985 and registered in Tiruchirappalli, Tamil Nadu, India.

Professor G. Sankaranarayanan was the first President, Professor R. Balakrishnan the first Secretary and Professor E. Sampathkumar the first Academic Secretary. The initial impetus for the formation of the Society was the deeply felt need of a new mathematical journal and the necessity of an organization to launch and nourish the journal.

The Ramanujan Mathematical Society's publications include the following:

- *Mathematics Newsletter:* A journal catering to the needs of students, research scholars, and teachers. The Newsletter was launched in the year 1991 with Professor R. Balakrishnan as Chief Editor. Currently, the Chief Editor is Professor S. Ponnusamy of the Indian Institute of Technology (IIT) Madras, Madras (now Chennai), India.
- *Journal of the Ramanujan Mathematical Society:* The Journal was started in 1986 with Professor K.S. Padmanabhan as Editor-in-Chief. Initially it was a biannual Journal, but now it has four issues per year. The present Editor-in-Chief is Professor R. Parimala of Emory University, Atlanta, USA and the Managing Editor is former Professor E Sampathkumar of University of Mysore, India.
- *Little Mathematical Treasures:* This is envisaged as a series of books addressed to mathematically mature readers and to bright students. A book, "Adventures in Iteration" by Dr Shailesh A Shirali, has been published under this series.
- *Ramanujan Mathematical Society Lecture Notes Series in Mathematics:* This is a series consisting of monographs and proceedings of the conferences, organized by the Ramanujan Mathematical Society.

The Society also organizes endowment lectures every year.

13.11 Ramanujan College, University of Delhi

Delhi University named one of its constituent colleges after Ramanujan, called Ramanujan College located in the South part of New Delhi and near South Campus of the University of Delhi, Delhi. The college has a large body of students studying various bachelor's courses in the disciplines of arts, commerce and science. Although the college offers many courses, its main focus has been on majors in mathematics, information technology, business studies, and psychology.

13.12 Museum on Ramanujan's life story

It is located in Chennai (formerly Madras), and has many photographs of Ramanujan's home and family, along with letters to and from friends, relatives, etc. The collection is the result of decades of efforts by late P.K. Srinivasan, a renowned mathematics teacher, who worked very hard for years looking for Ramanujan's pictures, letters, etc. that could be used in the museum. In 1993, he found a lot of material in a chest in Ramanujan's old attic.

13.13 Visiting Professorship Instituted at the University of California, Los Angeles, USA

India-born eminent mathematician Professor V.S. Varadarajan and his wife Veda have recently donated $1 million to the University of California at Los Angeles (UCLA) to establish a Visiting Professorship honoring legendary Srinivasa Ramanujan. It may be mentioned that Professor Varadarajan is at present Professor Emeritus in the Mathematics department of this university. This new position of Visiting Professor will help in attracting visiting faculty members in Professor Varadarajan's specializations of Automorphic Forms, which is an important concept in Number Theory, and linked to Elementary Particles and Quantum Physics.

□

14

Reference Material on Ramanujan

In this chapter, we give references to some of the work available on Ramanujan, which includes Ramanujan's Notebooks, Biographies and Books on Ramanujan, articles published on Ramanujan's life and his work, Ramanujan's published research papers, and his research papers published with G.H. Hardy.

14.1 Ramanujan's Notebooks

1. S. Ramanujan, *Notebooks. Vols. 1, 2,* Tata Institute of Fundamental Research, Bombay, 1957.
2. B.C. Berndt, *Ramanujan's Notebooks, Part I*, with a foreword by S. Chandrasekhar, Springer, New York, 1985. ISBN: 0-387-96110-0.
3. B.C. Berndt, *Ramanujan's Notebooks, Part II*, Springer, New York, 1989. ISBN: 0-387-96794-X;
4. B.C. Berndt, *Ramanujan's Notebooks, Part III*, Springer, New York, 1991. ISBN: 0-387-97503-9;
5. B.C. Berndt, *Ramanujan's Notebooks, Part IV*, Springer, New York, 1994. ISBN: 0-387-94109-6;
6. B.C. Berndt, *Ramanujan's Notebooks, Part V*, Springer, New York, 1998. ISBN: 0-387-94941-0;
7. S. Ramanujan, *The Lost Notebook and Other Unpublished Papers*, with an introduction by George E. Andrews, Springer, Berlin, 1988. ISBN: 3-540-18726-X.

14.2 Biographies and Books on Ramanujan

1. Biography in *Dictionary of Scientific Biography*, New York, 1970-1990.
2. Biography in *Encyclopaedia Britannica.*
3. Krishnaswami Alladi, *Ramanujan's Place in the World of Mathematics*, Springer, 2013.
4. B.C. Berndt and R.A. Rankin, *Ramanujan: Letters and Commentary*, (History of Mathematics, Vol 9), American Mathematical Society, Providence, Rhode Island, 1995.
5. N.K. Govil and Bhu Dev Sharma, *Adbhut Ganitigya Srinivasa Ramanujan (in Hindi), with an article on 'Srinivasa Ramanujan aur Ganit' by Dr. A.P.J. Abdul Kalam, former President of India*, Prabhat Prakashan, Delhi, India, first published in 2005, and multiple editions since then.
6. G.H. Hardy, *Ramanujan: Twelve Lectures on Subjects Suggested by His Life and Work*, AMS/ Chelsea Publishing, 1999.
7. G.H. Hardy, *Ramanujan*, Cambridge University Press, 1940.
8. G.H. Hardy, P.V. Seshu Aiyar and B.M. Wilson, *Collected papers of Srinivasa Ramanujan,* AMS Chelsea Publishing, American Mathematical Society, Providence, Rhode Island.
9. Robert Kanigel, *The Man Who Knew Infinity: A life of the genius Ramanujan*, Washington Square Press, 1992.
10. J.N. Kapur (ed.), *Some Eminent Indian Mathematicians of the Twentieth Century,* Mathematical Sciences Trust Society, 1983.
11. David Leavitt, *The Indian Clerk: A Novel,* Bloomsbury USA, 2007M.
12. Ram Murty, V. Kumar Murty, *The Mathematical Legacy of Srinivasa Ramanujan,* Springer, 2013.
13. Ken Ono, Amir D. Aczel, *My Search for Ramanujan: How I Learned to Count*, Springer, 2015.
14. S. Ram, *Srinivasa Ramanujan,* National Book Trust India, New Delhi, India, 2000.
15. S. Ramanujan, *Collected Papers,* Cambridge University Press, 1927.

16. S.R. Ranganathan, *Ramanujan: The Man and the Mathematician*, Asia Pub. House, Bombay, 1967.
17. William L. Shirer, *Gandhi: A Memoir*, Washington Square Press, 1982.
18. P.K. Srinivasan, *An Introduction to Creativity of Ramanujan,* Association of Mathematics Teachers of India, 1987.
19. Ian Stewart, *Significant Figures: The Lives and Work of Great Mathematicians,* Basic Books, 2017.

14.3 Articles published on Ramanujan's life and works

1. P.V. Seshu Aiyar, The late Mr. S. Ramanujan, B.A., F.R.S., *Journal of the Indian Mathematical Society,* **12** (1920), 81-86.
2. Krishnaswami Alladi, The SASTRA Ramanujan Prize: Its Origins and Its Winners, Notices Amer. Math. Soc., **66** (January 2019), 64-72.
3. G.E. Andrews, An introduction to Ramanujan's 'lost' notebook, *American Mathematical Monthly,* **86** (1979), 89-108.
4. B. Berndt, Srinivasa Ramanujan, *The American Scholar,* **58** (1989), 234-244.
5. B. Berndt and S. Bhargava, Ramanujan—For Lowbrows, *American Mathematical Monthly,* **100** (1993), 644-656.
6. B. Bollobas, Ramanujan—a glimpse of his life and his mathematics, *The Cambridge Review* (1988), 76-80.
7. B. Bollobas, Ramanujan—a glimpse of his life and his mathematics, *Eureka,* **48** (1988), 81-98.
8. J.M. Borwein and P.B. Borwein, Ramanujan and pi, *Scientific American,* **258** (2) (1988), 66-73.
9. S. Chandrasekhar, On Ramanujan: in *Ramanujan Revisited* (Proceedings of the Centenary Conference published by Academic Press), (1988), 1-6.
10. L. Debnath, Srinivasa Ramanujan (1887-1920): a centennial tribute, *International Journal of Mathematical Education in Science and Technology,* **18** (1987), 821-861.

11. G.H. Hardy, The Indian Mathematician Ramanujan, *American Mathematical Monthly,* **44** (3) (1937), 137-155.
12. G.H. Hardy, Srinivasa Ramanujan, *Proceedings of the London Mathematical Society,* **19** (1921), xl-lviii.
13. E H Neville, Srinivasa Ramanujan, *Nature,* **149** (1942), 292-294.
14. C.T. Rajagopal, Stray Thoughts on Srinivasa Ramanujan, *Mathematics Teacher (India)* **11A** (1975), 119-122, and **12** (1976), 138-139.
15. K. Ramachandra, Srinivasa Ramanujan (the inventor of the circle method), *Journal of Mathematics & Physical Sciences,* **21** (1987), 545-564.
16. K. Ramachandra, Srinivasa Ramanujan (the inventor of the circle method), *Hardy-Ramanujan J,* **10** (1987), 9-24.
17. R.A. Rankin, Ramanujan's Manuscripts and Notebooks, *Bulletin London Mathematical Society,* **14** (1982), 81-97.
18. R.A. Rankin, Ramanujan as a Patient, *Proceedings of the Indian Academy of Sciences,* **93** (1984), 79-100.
19. R.A. Rankin, Srinivasa Ramanujan (1887-1920), *International Journal of Mathematical Education in Science and Technology,* **18** (1987), 861.
20. R.A. Rankin, Ramanujan's manuscripts and notebooks II, *Bulletin of the London Mathematical Society,* **21** (1989), 351-365.
21. R. Ramachandra Rao, In Memoriam S. Ramanujan, B.A., F.R.S., *Journal of the Indian Mathematical Society,* **12** (1920), 87-90.
22. E. Shils, Reflections on Tradition, Centre and Periphery and the Universal Validity of Science: the Significance of the Life of S. Ramanujan," *Minerva,* **29** (1991), 393-419.
23. D.A.B. Young, Ramanujan's illness, *Notes and Records of the Royal Society of London,* **48** (1994), 107-119.

14.4 Published research papers of S. Ramanujan

1. Some Properties of Bernoulli's Numbers, *Journal of the Indian Mathematical Society,* **3** (1911), 219-234.

2. On Question 330 of Professor Sanjana, *Journal of the Indian Mathematical Society*, **4** (1912), 59-61.
3. Note on a Set of Simultaneous Equations, *Journal of the Indian Mathematical Society*, **5** (1913), 94-96.
4. Irregular Numbers, *Journal of the Indian Mathematical Society*, **5** (1913), 105-106.
5. Squaring the Circle, *Journal of the Indian Mathematical Society*, **5** (1913), 132.
6. Modular Equations and Approximation to π, *Quarterly Journal of Mathematics*, **45** (1914), 350–372.
7. On thc Integral $\int_0^x \frac{\tan^{-1} t}{t} dt$, *Journal of the Indian Mathematical Society*, **7** (1915), 93-96.
8. On the Number of Divisors of a Number, *Journal of the Indian Mathematical Society*, **7** (1915), 131-133.
9. On the Sum of Square Roots of First *n* Natural Numbers, *Journal of the Indian Mathematical Society*, **7** *(1915)*, 173-175.
10. On the Product $\prod_{n=0}^{n=\infty}\left[1+\left(\frac{x}{\text{Đ}+}\right)^3\right]$, *Journal of the Indian Mathematical Society*, **7** (1915), 209-211.
11. Some Definite integrals, *Messenger of Mathematics*, **44** (1915), 10-18
12. Some Definite Integrals Connected with Gauss's Sums, *Messenger of Mathematics*, **44** (1915), 75-85.
13. Summation of Certain Series, *Messenger of Mathematics*, **44** (1915), 157-160.
14. New Expressions for Riemann's Functions $\xi(s)$ *and* $\Xi(t)$, *Quarterly Journal of Mathematics*, **46** (1915), 253-260.
15. Highly Composite Numbers, *Proceedings of the London Mathematical Society*, **2** (1915), 347-409.
16. On Certain Infinite Series, *Messenger of Mathematics*, **45** (1916), 11-15.

17. Some Formulae in the Analytic Theory of Numbers, *Messenger of Mathematics,* **45** (1916), 81-84.
18. On Certain Arithmetical Functions, *Transactions of the Cambridge Philosophical Society,* **22,** 9 (1916), 159-184.
19. A Series for Euler's Constant γ, *Messenger of Mathematics,* **46** (1917), 73-80.
20. On the Expression of a Number in the form $ax^2+by^2+cz^2+du^2$, Proceedings *of the Cambridge Philosophical Society,* **19** (1917), 11-21.
21. On Certain Trigonometrical Sums and Their Applications in the Theory of Numbers, *Transactions of the Cambridge Philosophical Society,* **22** (1918), 259-276.
22. Some Definite Integrals, *Proceedings of the London Mathematical Society,* **2,** 17(1918), Records for 17th Jan. 1918
23. Some Definite Integrals, *Journal of the Indian Mathematical Society,* **11** (1919), 81-87.
24. A Proof of Bertrand's Postulate, *Journal of the Indian Mathematical Society,* **11** *(1919),* 181-82.
25. Some Properties of *p(n)*, the Number of Partitions of *n*, *Proceedings of the Cambridge Philosophical Society,* **19** (1919), 207-210.
26. Proofs of Certain Identities in Combinatorial Analysis, *Proceedings of the Cambridge Philosophical Society,* **19** (1919), 214-216.
27. A Class of Definite Integrals, *Quarterly Journal of Mathematics,* **48** (1920), 294-310.
28. Congruence Properties of Partitions, *Proceedings of the London Mathematical Society,* **2, 18** (1920), Records for 13th March 1919.
29. Algebraic Relations between Certain Infinite Products, *Proceedings of the London Mathematical Society,* **2, 18** (1920), Records for 13th March 1919
30. Congruence Properties of Partitions *Mathematische Zeitschrift,* **9** (1921), 147-153.

14.5 Ramanujan's Research Papers Jointly with G.H. Hardy

1. Une Formulae Asymptotique pour le Nombre des Partitions de *n*, *Comptes Rendus*, 2 Jan, 1917.
2. Proof that Almost All Numbers *n* are Composed about loglogn Prime Factors, *Proceedings of the London Mathematical Society*, **2, 16** (1917), Records for 14th Dec. 1916.
3. Asymptotic Formulae in Combinatorial Analysis, *Proceedings of the London Mathematical Society*, **2, 16** (1917), Records for 1st March 1917.
4. Asymptotic formulae for the Distribution of Integers of Various Types, *Proceedings of the London Mathematical Society*, **2, 16** (1917), 76-92.
5. The Normal Number of Prime Factors of a Number *n*, *Quarterly Journal of Mathematics*, **48** (1917), 76-92.
6. Asymptotic Formulae in Combinatorial Analysis, *Proceedings of the London Mathematical Society*, **2, 17** (1918), 75-115.
7. On the Coefficients in the Expansions of Certain Modular Functions, *Proceedings of the Royal Society*, A, **95** (1918), 144-155.

□

Appendix

The SASTRA Ramanujan Prize: Its Origins and Its Winners

—**Krishnaswami Alladi**

The SASTRA Ramanujan Prize is a $10,000 annual award given to mathematicians not exceeding the age of 32 for path-breaking contributions in areas influenced by the genius Srinivasa Ramanujan. The prize has been unusually effective in recognizing at an early stage in their careers, extremely gifted mathematicians who have gone on to accomplish even greater things in mathematics and be awarded prizes with a hallowed tradition such as the Fields Medal. This is due to the enthusiastic support from leading mathematicians around the world and the caliber of the winners. The age limit of 32 is because Ramanujan lived only for 32 years, and in that brief lifespan made revolutionary contributions;

Krishnaswami Alladi is professor of mathematics at the University of Florida, Gainesville. His email address is alladik@ufl.edu.

For permission to reprint this article, please contact: reprint permission@ams.org.

DOI: http://dx.doi.org/10.1090/noti1765

so the challenge for the prize candidates is to show what they have achieved in that same time frame! The way the prize was conceived and launched is an incredible story, which I will relate here. I will then briefly describe some major aspects of the work of the winners.

The Origins

The district of Tanjore (=*Tanjavur*) in the state of Tamil Nadu in South India has been a seat of culture for several centuries. Tanjore has produced some of greatest composers and performers of South Indian classical music. Ramanujan was born in Erode on 22 Dec, 1887, but it was in the Tanjore region steeped in culture that he lived in the town of Kumbakonam until he completed high school.

During the second half of the twentieth century, Ramanujan's humble home in Kumbakonam, from where a thousand theorems emerged, was in a dilapidated condi- tion. Even though in India, many events and programs were held regularly in Ramanujan's memory, including the grand Ramanujan Centenary celebrations in December 1987, nothing was done for the renovation of this historic home. One of the most significant developments in the worldwide effort to preserve and honor the legacy of Ramanujan is the purchase in 2003 of Ramanujan's home in Kumbakonam by SASTRA University to maintain it as a museum. This purchase had far-reaching consequences because it led to the involvement of a university in the preservation of Ramanujan's legacy for posterity.

The Shanmugha Arts, Science, Technology and Research Academy (SASTRA), is a private university in the town of Tanjore after which the district is named. SASTRA was founded in 1984 and has grown by leaps and bounds. Admission is very competitive, and SASTRA has succeeded in attracting some of the brightest students in India.

SASTRA has renovated Ramanujan's home beautifully without altering its structure or design. The only modifica- tion was to add a bust of Ramanujan in the living room. In connection with the purchase of Ramanujan's home, SASTRA University opened a branch campus in Kumbakonam in 2003, called the Srinivasa Ramanujan Centre. SASTRA has a museum there in which several important letters, photographs, and documents related to Ramanujan are displayed. A visit to Kumbakonam just to see Ramanujan's home and this museum will be worthwhile and inspiring.

One afternoon in September 2003, I received a phone call from S. Swaminathan, then a graduate student at the University of Virginia (now a dean at SASTRA). He introduced himself as the son of Vice-Chancellor R. Sethuraman of SASTRA University, gave me some background about SASTRA, and said that to mark the occasion of the purchase of Ramanujan's home, SASTRA would be conducting an international conference that year in December at the Kumbakonam campus. The President of India, Dr. Abdul Kalam, had agreed to inaugurate this conference on December 20, 2003 and declare Ramanujan's home as a national treasure. Swaminathan invited me to bring a team of mathematicians from abroad to the conference, and said that SASTRA would cover all their expenses including international travel. I felt that what I heard over the phone was incredible because international airfare is rarely paid for mathematical conferences in India. But on checking, I realized that something important was taking place. So I called George Andrews of Pennsylvania State University, the world's foremost authority in the theory of partitions and on Ramanujan's work, told him about SASTRA, and requested that he come to the conference. He said that, based on my assurance, he would come. In fact, Andrews gave the opening lecture of the conference as well as the concluding Ramanujan Commemoration Lecture on December 22, Ramanujan's birthday. At the valedictory function, the participants suggested that SASTRA should conduct conferences annually around Ramanujan's birthday on different areas of mathematics influenced by Ramanujan. Dean Vaidhyasubramaniam of SASTRA agreed to this suggestion and invited me to help organize these annual conferences. I have done this annually since 2003, and so have also had the pleasure of being in Ramanujan's hometown each year in December thus making it an annual pilgrimage for me (see article 25 in [1], pp. 153–160).

For the second SASTRA Ramanujan Conference in 2004, the Vice-Chancellor invited me to inaugurate it and also deliver the concluding Ramanujan Commemoration lecture. I was honored to get such an invitation, and I accepted it happily.

Figure 1. *Krishna Alladi being introduced to the President of India, Dr. Abdul Kalam, during the First Ramanujan Conference at SASTRA University on December 20, 2003.To the left of Krishna are George Andrews (Penn State) and Noam Elkies (Harvard).*

Conference inaugurations in India are usually elaborate and grand ceremonies starting with the traditional "lighting of the lamp" by the Chief Guest, with the lamp representing enlightenment through knowledge. There was a large gathering in the auditorium, and as we walked up to the stage to be seated before the official start of the ceremony, the Vice-Chancellor whispered to me and said, "I wish to give $10,000 annually for a worthy cause in the name of Ramanujan. You please decide how it should be used and announce it in your inaugural speech". I was pleasantly shocked by this and said, "This is very generous of you, but are you asking me to announce this in the next few minutes without consulting anybody?" He said, "Yes, consulting people, or going through a Committee, will cause unnecessary delays, and so I want you to come to decision right now and announce it". Fortunately, my inaugural speech was preceded by the lamp lighting ceremony and the customary elaborate welcome of the audience and the introduction of the Chief Guest (me) as is common in India, and so I had at least fifteen minutes to think about it as all this was going on! When I got up to speak, I mentioned this very generous offer from the Vice-Chancellor, and suggested that a SASTRA Ramanujan Prize be created and that $10,000 be given to a mathematician not exceeding the age of 32 for outstanding contributions to areas influenced by Ramanujan. I pointed out that the Fields Medal is given only to those under 40 years of age, and the SASTRA Prize would be given to even younger mathematicians, some of whom may later win the Fields Medal or other well-established major prizes. The Vice-Chancellor liked this suggestion very much, and at the conclusion of the inaugural ceremony, in thanking me, he confirmed that the prize would be launched the next year. He then turned towards me and said, "I request you to be the Chair of the Prize Committee". So that is how the SASTRA Ramanujan Prize was conceived and launched, and how I got involved with the Prize. All this happened within the span of an hour during the inauguration.

Upon return to the United States, I called George Andrews and told him this incredible story of the launch of the prize and said that for this to be a success, I would need the support of the mathematical community. In particular, I wanted his presence on the Committee for the first year. He was surprised and happy to hear this and agreed to serve on the Prize Committee. Over the years, eminent mathematicians have supported the prize by either serving on the Prize Committee, making nominations, or writing letters evaluating the work of the nominees. The prize is given annually at SASTRA University, Kumbakonam, during an international conference held around Ramanujan's birthday.

The winners

The 2005 Prizes: Manjul Bhargava of Princeton University and Kannan Soundararajan of the University of Michigan came out on top as the strongest young mathematicians in the areas of algebraic number theory and analytic number theory, respectively, and were equally ranked 1 by the Committee.

One of the pioneering discoveries of Gauss was the composition law for binary quadratic forms. Introducing several new and unexpected ideas, Bhargava broke an impasse since the time of Gauss, and established in his 2001 PhD thesis at Princeton University composition laws for higher degree forms. Bhargava applied these to solve new cases of one of the fundamental questions of number theory that of the asymptotic enumeration of number fields of a given degree. He published the results in his thesis in a series of papers in the *Annals of Mathematics*. Bhargava's lecture at SASTRA University upon accepting the prize was on a different topic; he announced his joint work with Jonathan Hanke on the solution of the problem of determining all universal quadratic forms—a problem whose origin can be traced back to Ramanujan.

Kannan Soundararajan had made spectacular contributions to analytic number theory, most notably pertaining to the Riemann zeta function and Dirichlet L-functions— especially on the distribution and location of their zeros. He also established deep results in random matrix theory, which has fundamental connections with prime number theory. In his PhD thesis at Princeton University, he showed that 7/8-ths of the quadratic L-functions have no zeros at the critical point $s = 1/2$, which provided strong evidence for a certain conjecture of Chowla. Along with Brian Conrey, he had shown that a positive proportion of Dirichlet L-functions have no zeros on the real axis within the critical strip.

Figure 2. *Kannan Soundararajan (then at Michigan) receiving the first SASTRA Ramanujan Prize on December 20, 2005 from Dr. Arabinda Mitra, Director, Department of Science and Technology, India. (Second from Left) Manjul Bhargava (Princeton) who had received the same prize a few minutes earlier, looks on. Next to Mitra is SASTRA Vice-Chancellor R. Sethuraman, and next to Soundararajan is Krishna Alladi.*

The Prize Committee felt that both candidates deserved the full award. The SASTRA Vice-Chancellor generously agreed to the recommendation of the Committee that Bhargava and Soundararajan be awarded two full prizes, and that it should not be split. Thus, the SASTRA Ramanujan Prize could not have had a better start (see Ken Ono's article [3] on the award of the first SASTRA Ramanujan Prizes, and mine ([1], p. 161-166) as well).

Bhargava continued producing fundamental work after receiving the SASTRA Ramanujan Prize, especially related to the average rank of elliptic curves. He was recognized with the AMS Cole Prize in 2008 and the Fields Medal in 2014.

When Soundararajan received the SASTRA Prize, he was a tenured faculty member at Michigan, and in the next year, was appointed full professor at Stanford. Subsequently, he was recognized with the Infosys Prize and the Ostrowski Prize, both in 2011.

The 2006 Prize: Thirty-one-year-old Terence Tao of UCLA had made far-reaching contributions to diverse areas of mathematics such as number theory, harmonic analysis, partial differential equations, and ergodic theory. He was widely regarded as one of the most influential mathematicians of our time.

One of Tao's most notable contributions was for the Kakeya Problem in higher dimensions. One aspect of the problem is to determine the fractal dimension of a set obtained by rotating a needle in n-dimensional space. In joint work with Nets Katz, Isabella Laba, and others, he improved all previously known estimates for the fractal dimension with ingenious combinatorial ideas. Another of Tao's seminal contributions was his joint work with Ben Green on long arithmetic progressions of prime numbers. One of the deepest results in this area is due to the Hungarian mathematician Szemerédi who showed that any set of positive density will have arbitrarily long arithmetic progressions. Subsequently Tim Gowers of Cambridge University gave a very different proof of Szemerédi's theorem. This result of Szemerédi does not apply to the set of primes, which is of zero density. By combining the ideas of Gowers along with tools from ergodic theory, Green and Tao proved the sensational result that there are arbitrarily long arithmetic progressions of primes.

Figure 3. *Krishna Alladi reads the citation before the 2006 SASTRA Ramanujan Prize is presented to Terence Tao (standing, middle) of UCLA.*

Yet another fundamental contribution of Tao concerns the sum-product problem due to Paul Erdös and Szemerédi. Roughly speaking, this problem states that either the sum set or the product set of a set of *N* numbers must be large. Tao was the first to recognize the significance of this problem in combinatorial number theory and harmonic analysis. In collaboration with Nets Katz and Jean Bourgain, Tao made important generalizations that led to breakthroughs in harmonic analysis and number theory.

Honors have come to him in a steady stream. In 2006, Tao was awarded both the Fields Medal and the SASTRA Ramanujan Prize. More recently, he received the 2014 Breakthrough Prize. He currently holds the James and Carol Collins Chair at UCLA.

The 2007 Prize: Ben Green of Cambridge University had made phenomenal contributions to several fundamental problems in number theory by himself and in collaboration with Terence Tao. Green's PhD thesis at Cambridge is a collection of several outstanding papers. In one of these papers he solved the Cameron- Erdös conjecture, which is a bound on the number of sum-free sets of positive integers up to a given number *N* Green had also established an important result that any set of primes with relative positive density would contain infinitely many arithmetic progressions of length 3. It was this paper of Green in the 2005 *Annals of Mathematics* that caught the attention of Tao and which led to their collaborative and definitive result on arbitrarily long arithmetic progressions among the primes. Subsequently Green and Tao also collaborated in extending the Hardy-Ramanujan-Littlewood Circle Method by bringing in methods from ergodic theory.

Figure 4. *2007 SASTRA Prize Winner Ben Green (then at Cambridge University) seated on the windowsill of the bedroom at Ramanujan's home.The cot there was the only one for Ramanujan's family. As a boy, Ramanujan used to sit on the windowsill and do his "sums" watching the passers-by on the street.*

In 2005, Green was appointed Hershel Smith Professor at Cambridge University. He was elected Fellow of the Royal Society in 2010 and was awarded the Sylvester Medal in 2014. He is currently Waynflete Professor of Pure Mathematics at Oxford University.

The 2008 Prize: Akshay Venkatesh of Stanford University was creating waves in the mathematical world by making powerful contributions to diverse areas, by himself and with a host of collaborators. His 2006 paper with H. Helf- gott contained striking and original ideas, and provided the first non-trivial upper bound for the 3-torsion in class groups of quadratic fields. His joint work with Jordan Ellen berg on representing integral quadratic forms by quadratic forms had its roots in the work of Ramanujan.

***Figure 5.** Akshay Venkatesh (Stanford), 2008 SASTRA Prize Winner, garlanding the statue of Ramanujan at SASTRA University.*

An important and difficult problem in number theory is to asymptotically count number fields according to their discriminant. The case up to degree 5 had been solved by Manjul Bhargava. For large degrees, Ellenberg and Venkatesh provided the first major improvement over bounds in earlier work of Wolfgang Schmidt and thus broke an impasse of thirty years. Also of great importance was Venkatesh's work on sub-convexity of automorphic *L*-functions, and his joint work with E. Lindenstrauss, which settled a famous conjecture of Peter Sarnak concerning locally symmetric spaces.

After the SASTRA Ramanujan Prize, he has been awarded the Infosys Prize in 2016 and the Ostrowski Prize in 2017. In 2018, he was awarded the Fields Medal and appointed to the permanent faculty at the Institute for Advanced Study, Princeton.

The 2009 Prize: The 2009 Prize was awarded to Kathrin Bringmann for work related to Ramanujan's mock theta functions. A good portion of Ramanujan's Lost Notebook, namely, the loose sheets of paper on which he wrote hundreds of formulas shortly before he died in 1920, is devoted to mock theta functions. These are objects that are like the classical theta functions in their shape, but are not modular forms, yet their coefficients can be calculated with a degree of precision comparable to what can be done for functions that can be expressed in terms of theta func- tions. No one knew the exact relationship between theta functions and mock theta functions, and indeed determining this relationship was one of the tantalizing puzzles of mathematics. Following a lead provided by Sander Zwegers, Kathrin Bringmann and her post-doctoral mentor Ken Ono provided the key to unlock this mystery by showing how mock theta functions are intimately connected with harmonic Maass forms.

***Figure 6.** 2009 SASTRA Prize Winner Kathrin Bringmann (University of Cologne) lighting the ceremonial lamp to mark the opening of the Ramanujan Conference.*

The 2010 Prize: As a PhD student at Columbia University, Wei Zhang had made seminal contributions by himself and in collaboration with others to a broad range of areas in mathematics including number theory, automorphic forms, trace formulas, L-functions, representation theory, and algebraic geometry.

In 1997, Steve Kudla constructed a family of cycles on Shimura varieties, and conjectured that their generating functions are actually Siegel modular forms. The proof of the Kudla conjecture for cycles of codimension 1 is a major theorem of Fields Medalist Richard Borcherds. In his PhD thesis, Zhang established conditionally, among other things, a generalization of Borcherds'result for higher dimensions and in that process essentially settled the Kudla conjecture. Zhang's thesis opened up major lines of research and led to significant colaboration with Xinyi Yuan and Shouwu Zhang. The three established an arithmetic analogue of a theorem of Waldspurger that connects Integral periods to values of L-functions. In addition, Wei Zhang by himself had done outstanding work on relative trace formulas, and on Shimura varieties.

When Zhang received the SASTRA Prize, he was Benjamin Pierce Instructor at Harvard. In 2017, he was awarded the New Horizons Prize in Mathematics. He is currently a full professor at Columbia University.

***Figure 7.** 2010 SASTRA Prize Winner Wei Zhang (then at Harvard) seated (on the right) along with his former PhD advisor Shouwu Zhang (Columbia) at the entrance to Ramanujan's home in Kumbakonam.*

The 2011 Prize: Roman Holowinsky of Ohio State University had made significant contributions at the interface of analytic number theory and the theory of modular forms. Along with Kannan Soundararajan he solved an important case of the famous Quantum Unique Ergodicity (QUE) Conjecture. This was a spectacular achievement.

In 1991, Zeev Rudnick and Peter Sarnak formulated the QUE Conjecture, which in its general form concerns the correspondence principle for quantizations of chaotic systems. One aspect of the problem is to understand how waves are influenced by the geometry of their enclosure. Rudnick and Sarnak conjectured that for sufficiently chaotic systems, if the surface has negative curvature, then the high frequency quantum wave functions are uniformly distributed within the domain. The modular domain in number theory is one of the most important examples, and for this case, Holowinsky and Soundararajan solved the holomorphic QUE conjecture.

The manner in which this solution came about is amazing. By a study of Hecke eigenvalues and an ingenious application

***Figure 8.** 2011 SASTRA Prize Winner Roman Holowinsky (Ohio State) delivering the Ramanujan Commemoration Lecture on December 22, Ramanujan's birthday.*

of the sieve, Holowinsky obtained critical estimates for shifted convolution sums and this almost settled the holomorphic QUE conjecture for the modular domain except in certain cases where the corresponding L-functions behave abnormally. Simultaneously, Soundararajan approached the problem from an entirely different direction, was able to confirm the conjecture in several cases, and noticed that the exceptional cases not fitting Holowinsky's approach were covered by his techniques. Thus, by combining the approaches of Holowinsky and Soundararajan, the holomorphic QUE Conjecture was fully resolved in the modular case.

The 2012 Prize: Zhiwei Yun of Stanford University had made fundamental contributions to areas that lie at the interface of representation theory, algebraic geometry, and number theory. Yun's PhD thesis on global Springer theory at Princeton University opened up new vistas in the Langlands program. Springer theory is the study of Weyl group actions on the cohomology of certain subvarieties of the flag manifold called Springer fibers. Yun's global Springer theory deals with Hitchin fibers instead of Springer fibers, which he used to determine the actions of affine Weyl groups on cohomology.

Bao-Châu Ngô was awarded the 2010 Fields Medal for his proof of the Fundamental Lemma in the Langlands Program. Yun made a breakthrough in the study of the Fundamental Lemma formulated by Jacquet and Rallis in their program of proving the Gross–Prasad conjecture on relative trace formulas. Yun's understanding of Hitchin fibrations enabled him to reduce the Jacquet–Rallis fundamental lemma to a cohomological property of the Hitchin fibration. In addition, Yun's work on the uniform construction of motives with exceptional Galois groups is considered to be very fundamental.

Since 2012 was the 125th Birth Anniversary of Ramanujan, Yun was awarded the SASTRA Prize in India's capital New Delhi, at a conference organized by the National Board for Higher Mathematics (of India), and co-sponsored by SASTRA University and Delhi University. That was the only year when this prize was not awarded in Kumbakonam.

Figure 9. *Zhiwei Yun (MIT and Stanford) receiving the 2012 SASTRA Ramanujan Prize from Minister of State Jitin Prasada at the University of Delhi on December 22. SASTRA Vice-Chancellor Sethuraman and Krishna Alladi are looking on.*

When Yun received the SASTRA Prize, he had just been appointed to the permanent faculty at Stanford University after having completed his term as Moore Instructor at MIT. In 2018, he was a recipient of the New Horizons in Mathematics Prize.

The 2013 Prize: Peter Scholze of the University of Bonn had made revolutionary contributions to arithmetic algebraic geometry and the theory of automorphic forms. Already in his Masters thesis at Bonn, Scholze gave a new proof of the Local Langlands Conjecture for general linear groups based on a novel approach to calculate the zeta function of certain algebraic varieties. While this was groundbreaking, his PhD thesis at Bonn was a much bigger breakthrough: he developed a new p-adic machine called *perfectoid spaces* and used it brilliantly to prove a significant part of the weighted monodromy conjecture due to Deligne, thereby breaking an impasse of more than 30 years. Scholze extended his theory of perfectoid spaces to develop a Hodge theory for rigid analytic spaces over p-adic ground fields, generalizing a theory due to Faltings for algebraic varieties.

***Figure 10.** (L to R) 2013 SASTRA Prize Winner Peter Scholze (University of Bonn) and his former PhD Advisor Michael Rappoport (Bonn) standing next to the statue of Ramanujan at SASTRA University.*

Scholze was the youngest winner of the SASTRA Prize at the age of 25. Following that, he has been recognized with the AMS Cole Prize (2015), the Fermat Prize (2015), the Ostrowski Prize (2015), the Leibniz Prize (2016), and the Fields Medal (2018).

The 2014 Prize: James Maynard of Oxford University, England, and of the University of Montreal, had made outstanding contributions to some of the most famous problems on prime numbers. He obtained the strongest results at the time on the celebrated prime twins conjecture by showing that the gap between consecutive primes does not exceed 600 infinitely often. Not only did he significantly improve the path-breaking work of Goldston, Pintz, Yıldırım, and Zhang, but he achieved it with ingenious methods that were simpler than those used by others.

A generalization of the prime twins conjecture is the prime k-tuples conjecture, which states that an admissible collection of k linear functions will simultaneously take k prime values infinitely often. In the last one hundred years, several partial results towards the k-tuples conjecture were obtained by replacing prime values with "almost primes," namely numbers with a bounded number of prime factors. Another major achievement of Maynard was to significantly improve on the work of earlier researchers on k-tuples of almost primes.

Just before receiving the SASTRA Prize, Maynard announced the solution to the famous $10,000 problem of Erdös on large gaps between primes. This was simultaneously announced by Kevin Ford, Ben Green, Sergei Konyagin, and Terence Tao, but Maynard's method was different and simpler. Maynard's results and methods have led to a resurgence of activity worldwide in prime number theory.

***Figure 11.** James Maynard (Oxford University), the 2014 SASTRA Prize Winner, standing next to the Ramanujan statue at SASTRA University.*

After the SASTRA Prize, he received the Whitehead Prize in 2015 and the EMS Prize in 2016. He is currently a professor at Magdalen College, Oxford University.

The 2015 Prize: Jacob Tsimerman of the University of Toronto had made deep and original contributions to diverse parts of number theory, most notably to the André-Oort Conjecture, which states that special subsets of Shimura varieties that are obtained as Zariski closures of special points are finite unions of Shimura varieties. Shimura varieties are special algebraic varieties (such as moduli spaces of abelian varieties) that arise as quotients of suitable complex domains by arithmetic groups. Yves André initially stated this conjecture for one-dimensional sub-varieties, and subsequently Frans Oort proposed that it should hold more generally. A major achievement of Tsimerman in his Princeton PhD thesis of 2011 was to obtain certain unconditional bounds up to dimension 6. Another important result in his thesis was to answer in the affirmative a question of Nick Katz and Oort whether there exists an abelian variety over the set of all algebraic numbers that is not isogenous to the Jacobian of a stable algebraic curve over the algebraic numbers.

Figure 12. *2015 SASTRA Prize Winner Jacob Tsimerman (University of Toronto) standing outside Ramanujan's home.The majestic Gopuram (entrance tower) of the Sarangapani Temple, where Ramanujan and family regularly worshipped, is seen in the background.*

Just before receiving the SASTRA Prize, Tsimerman gave a proof of the André-Oort Conjecture for the moduli spaces of principally polarized abelian varieties of any dimension—a result that was sought for a long time.

The 2016 Prize: This was shared by Kaisa Matomäki of

the University of Turku, Finland, and Maksym Radziwill of McGill University, Canada, and Rutgers University. Their revolutionary collaborative work on multiplicative functions in short intervals shocked the mathematical community by going well beyond what could be proved previously even assuming the Riemann Hypothesis, and opened the door for a series of breakthroughs on some notoriously difficult questions such as the Erdös discrepancy problem and Chowla's conjecture, previously believed to be well beyond reach. Their stunning work on multiplicative functions in short intervals is best illustrated in terms of the Liouville lambda function, which takes value 1 when an integer has an even number of prime factors (counted with multiplicity), and value -1 at an integer with an odd number of prime factors. The statement that the lambda function takes values 1 and -1 with asymptotically equal frequency is equivalent to the Prime Number Theorem; more refined statements on the relative error in this equal frequency are related to the Riemann Hypothesis. Such equal distribution results were known also for short intervals, namely intervals $[x, x+h]$, where h is a fractional power (<1) of x. The Riemann Hypothesis implies that powers of h larger than 1/2 will work. Instead of every interval of length h, if we require only "almost all" intervals of length h, it was known that h could be made as small as the 1/6- th power of x, and as small as a power of $\log x$ by assuming the Riemann Hypothesis. Matomäki and Radziwill shocked the world by showing unconditionally that equal frequency holds almost always as long as h tends to infinity with x.

Figure 13. *Maksym Radziwill (McGill University) giving the Ramanujan Commemmoration Lecture on his joint work with Kaisa Matomäki with whom he shared the 2016 SASTRA Prize.*

Figure 14. *Kaisa Matomäki.*

Sarvadaman Chowla conjectured that if any k collection of values of 1 and -1 are given in any order, then the lambda function will take that sequence of values at k consecutive integers with asymptotic frequency $1/2^k$. This conjecture is yet unsolved. In 2016, Matomäki, Radziwill, and Terence Tao proved that when $k = 3$, each of the eight sign choices occur with positive proportion.

The 2017 Prize: Maryna Viazovska of the Swiss Federal Institute of Technology, Lausanne, was awarded the 2017 SASTRA Prize for her stunning solution in dimension 8 of the sphere-packing problem, and for her equally impressive joint work with Henry Cohn, Abhinav Kumar, Stephen D. Miller, and Danylo Radchenko, resolving the sphere-packing problem in dimension 24, by building upon her fundamental ideas in dimension 8.

The sphere-packing problem has a long and illustrious history. Johannes Kepler asked for the optimal way to stack cannon balls (of uniform radius) and conjectured a configuration, but could not prove it. This Kepler Conjecture was resolved by Thomas Hales in 1998 by combining ingenious geometric optimization arguments with machine calculations. The sphere-packing problem in higher dimensions remained open.

In dimension 8 there is E_8, an exceptional Lie group with a root lattice of rank 8, and in dimension 24 there is the Leech lattice. This gave some hope that the sphere-packing problem could be solved in dimensions 8 and 24. Noam Elkies and Henry Cohn made significant progress and conjectured the existence of certain magic auxiliary functions in dimensions 8 and 16, which, if determined, would resolve the conjecture in these dimensions. Viazovska produced these functions in dimension 8 by ingenious use of modular forms. Her proof is remarkably simple. Within a span of week, working at a furious pace, by extending the ideas in dimension 8, the sphere-packing problem in dimension 24 was resolved by Cohn, Kumar, Miller, Radchenko, and Viazovska.

Figure 15. *(L to R) Henry Cohn (Microsoft Research) discussing with 2017 SASTRA Prize Winner Maryna Viazovska (EPF Lausanne) and Ken Ono (Emory)*

In 2018, Viazovska was also awarded the New Horizons in Mathematics Prize.

Shaping the development of mathematics: The Fields Medals, with an age limit of 40 for the winners, were instituted with two lofty goals in mind: (i) to recognize pioneering work by brilliant young mathematicians, and (ii) to encourage these young researchers to continue to influence the growth of mathematics. The Fields Medalists have lived up to these great expectations. The SASTRA Ramanujan Prize has a more stringent age limit of 32, and so has recognized brilliant mathematicians even earlier in their careers. It is no exaggeration to say that the winners of the SASTRA Ramanujan Prizes have also shaped the development of mainstream mathematics and will continue to do so in the years ahead; the fact that the SASTRA laureates have subsequently won major prizes is a testimony to this.

Indeed, two of the four 2018 Fields Medalists are former SASTRA Ramanujan Prize Winners: Akshay Venkatesh and Peter Scholze! Similarly, three of the four 2018 New Horizons in Mathematics Prize winners are former SASTRA awardees: Wei Zhang, Zhiwei Yun, and Maryna Viazovska.

References

1. Alladi K, *Ramanujan's place in the world of mathematics—essays providing a comparative study*, Springer, New Delhi (2012), 177 pp.
2. Alladi K, "Ramanujan's thriving legacy," in Srinivasa Ramanujan going strong at 125, Parts I and II, *Notices Amer. Math. Soc.*, **I: 59** (2012), 1522-1537; **II: 60** (2013), 10–22. MR3027107 and MR3052461
3. Ono K, Honoring a gift from Kumbakonam, *Notices Amer. Math. Soc.*, June–July 2006, 641–651. MR2235326

Credits

Figure 9 is courtesy of SASTRA.

Figure 14 is by Pekka Matomäki.

All other article photos and author photo are courtesy of the Krishnaswami Alladi.

The 2018 SASTRA Ramanujan Prize is shared by Yifeng Liu (Yale University) and Jack Thorne (Cambridge University) for spectacular contributions to algebraic geometry, automorphic representations and number theory.

See p.113 of this issue for the Math People announcement about the 2018 SASTRA Prize to Liu and Thorne.

□

Index

J

K

L

O

P

R

S

□□□